HER PLUS ONE

A THANKSGIVING ROMANCE

S. CASSADERA

MAJOR KEY
KEY
PUBLISHING

SYNOPSIS

Nursing a broken heart days before her cousin's wedding leaves Aurora questioning her worth. It's a good thing her best friend has her best intentions at heart. While on this trip, they encounter miscommunication of their lips. What happens at the reception indeed stays at the reception, right?

Well, Malcolm has been in love with his best friend for over a decade. While her ex tries to sneak his way back into her heart, he takes his chance.

Will their forbidden relationship be tested during the holiday, or will they return to being friends for a happily ever after?

This holiday novella is a slow-burn story, packed with tense moments, laughter, desire, and lots of festivities.

PREFACE

Happy Fall Y'all/Thanksgiving!

Hello readers, thanks for taking the time to download or purchase this short story filled with the gift of loving your best friend. Before you get started reading, it's best if you start listening to DSVN "Think About Me." It sets the mood for the story. Better yet, listen to his whole album, lol.

This is a sweet, not steamy romance. If you like Hallmark movies, then you'll appreciate this. Anywho, y'all ready to have a good time reading by the fireplace, on the sofa with a cup of coffee or tea in your hands, or your own comfort spot? If so, dive in and tell me what you think afterward.

Happy Reading!
S. Cassadera

NOVELLA PLAYLIST

DSVN-Think About Me
Lauryn Hill-Can't Take My Eyes off You
Raheem Devaughn-Guess Who Loves You More
Vedo-You Got It
Wale-The Matrimony
Eraykah Badu-Love of My Life
Gourdan Banks-Keep you in Mind
Shai-If I Ever Fall in Love
October Marvin-Back to Your Place
Luke James-These Arms/Stay with me
Boys II Men-Bended Knees
Daniel Casear-Always
Mary J Blige-Sweet Thing
DaBaby-Shake Sumn
Young Dro-Shoulder Lean
Raheem Devaughn-Black Ice Cream
Juvenile-Back That Thang Up
Snoh Aalegra-I Want You Around

DSVN-Hallucinations
Major-This Is Why I Love You

ONE

THE BEGINNING

Aurora

"I can't do this anymore?"

"Do what?" I asked, stepping out of the shower we just shared.

Marshon stopped in the middle of the bedroom with the towel wrapped around his muscular waist and pointed his accusatory finger between us. "This," he snapped as he searched for a pair of black boxer briefs from the top drawer.

I looked at my boyfriend of three years like he'd lost his mind. What did he imply we couldn't do this? "What are you talking about?" Wrapping the towel firmly around my breast, I sat on the edge of the bed and tried to grasp what he was telling me.

Marshon steadied himself by grabbing on the edge of the dresser and stepping inside the underwear. Straightening his posture, he curled his upper lip. "See, there you go acting like you don't know what's been going on."

I held up my hand but realized it was shaking. I lowered it

immediately. I didn't want Marshon to know I was nervous despite the trembling. I couldn't wrap my head around his confession. What was happening? A few minutes ago, everything seemed peachy-king. But now?

Swaying his head, he marched to the closet and pulled out a duffle bag. He started stuffing the few clothes he had inside.

"'Shon, are you freaking serious right now?"

"Very."

I pointed toward the bathroom. "What was that a few minutes ago?" The pitch in my voice elevated.

He looked up and smiled. "I guess a proper goodbye."

I tried not to let his nonchalant attitude get to me. Calmly, I asked, "If you knew the end of tonight, then why go there with me?"

"For old-time sake." The arrogance in his voice was bold.

Feeling used, I jumped to my feet defensively and moved aggressively toward my phone.

"What are you doing?" I heard from behind me.

"What I always do," I angrily blurted, lifting my phone to my face.

The moment I felt his commanding presence behind me, I knew it before I could react. Marshon snatched the phone and held it captive behind his back. "That's your damn problem!" he hollered, his tone increased.

I instantly faced him, narrowing my eyes and folding my arms. "What does that supposed to mean?"

He flicked his wrist. "You're always running to him like he's your man instead of me."

Clapping my hands irked him. And I didn't care at the moment because he didn't care about mine. "News flash, you're not my man," I said, twisting my neck with an attitude. "And if I decide to call my best friend, then so be it. You don't get to tell me what to do anymore. Now give me my phone back," I extended my hand, waiting.

His dark eyes deepened. His face contorted. Nodding his head with a smirk, he removed the phone from behind his back.

Within reach, I seized the phone and went to my shortcut, tapping 'BFF' from my contacts list.

While he blatantly ignored me, Marshon continued packing his belongings.

I turned my back from him as I placed the phone on the dresser, pulling a long tee shirt from another drawer. I dropped the towel and pulled it over my body.

"What's up?"

"Hey, Mal---" Before I could get another word out, Marshon nabbed the phone from my grip once again. "What the hell?"

He ended the call. "He will always be your problem if you don't learn to let him go."

Learn to let him go. He was my best friend! I jerked my neck and arched my brows because I was beside myself. I would argue with anyone about my best friend. To me, Malcolm was never the problem. He was my confidante and supporter. As I thought to tell Marshon about himself, my phone started ringing. We both looked down at the nickname I saved under his name.

He chuckled bitterly. "BFF...huh? Yeah, I wonder why I was never called that."

I side-eyed him. He knew he wasn't my BFF. Just the bf, well, he was.

As I heard the phone ring, Marshon's offensive words echoed repeatedly. *Learn to let him go.* When I lifted my eyes to his, I felt remorseful of something, maybe this dead-end relationship.

Marshon was fully dressed in pants and a shirt as he lowered his head. "Hey, maybe this time apart will do both of us some good." He grabbed my hands as he spoke. "I know I would like for us to be friends again. Or who knows...maybe we'll hook back up in the future, but I need this time to sort out my plans. I need to evaluate where I need to be in life."

"Just not with me, huh." A smirk slipped from my face.

He lifted my chin. "It's more than that, and you know it. In the back of my mind, it'll always be him," he complained like a big kid not getting his way.

"What about Colorado?"

Marshon released my hands and stepped back. "I'll get a credit and go somewhere else. But in the meantime, you got your best friend." He winked playfully. He lifted a couple of bags from the floor onto his broad shoulder. "I'll be back."

Staring at the back of Marshon's head, my gaze shifted to the floor. I didn't know how long I stared, but Marshon's voice interrupted my trance.

"Are you going to get that?" he inquired, walking over to a black duffle bag on the floor by the dresser.

Nodding, I lifted my head from the floor and answered the phone.

"Hey, what's going on? Is everything okay?" Malcolm asked desperately.

My lips parted, but Marshon walked toward me with a crooked smile. With the duffle bag attached to his shoulder, he tenderly kissed me on the forehead and exited the bedroom.

"Aurora? You there?" Malcolm asked repeatedly.

I answered weakly, "He left me." I didn't know if Malcolm could tell I was broken from the few words I spoke, but his reassuring voice told me he'd see me shortly. I suddenly collapsed on the bed. The shock of tonight was too much for tears. I felt like my whole world was crashing in. Another failed relationship. *Why weren't the men happy with me?*

Malcolm didn't fail in his mission as he entered my home, calling my nickname 'Rory'.

I figured I didn't have any passion in my voice to greet him the same way so I said nothing. I knew sooner or later, he'd find me. There was a soft knock on the bedroom door. I turned my body away from Malcolm's view.

"Hey, what's wrong?" His mellow voice was soothing, soft, and silky. I knew him like the back of my hand and vice versa. He was standing by the doorway, taking off his shoes and setting them in the corner. As Marshon once hinted, *'Y'all are extremely too close, possessing a key to each other place'*. Reminiscing about the memory pulled a faint smile from me.

We met my freshman year of college. I was in search of the science building. Once I located it, I had to find the number to the classroom. I walked up and down the hallway unable to find it. And I hated to ask people for help. Numerous people were standing around. Instead of asking someone, I walked to the room and glanced at the number. It was 7348, but I was looking for 7384. When I backpedaled, I ran into a solid body. The body belonged to a nice-looking man with reddish brown skin and dark eyes. He was standing in a group of two women and another guy.

With a lopsided grin, I apologize. "I'm sorry," I stated meekly, head lowered.

"Hey, it's no big deal. Everyone makes mistakes." His tone was playful.

I lifted my head, and my pupils dilated. His eyes were a mirror to my soul. Smiling nervously, I glanced awkwardly behind me and turned in several directions.

Giving me a lazy smile, he asked, "Are you lost?"

I nodded. "Can you tell?"

He chuckled. "Yeah. If you want, I can help you look for your class."

It was a sweet gesture but I couldn't allow him to walk me to class and be tardy with his own. I tried to refuse his offer but the sudden arm overlapping my shoulder and grabbing my schedule from my hand gave me my answer.

"Your class is on the opposite side of the hallway."

That's when he became my best friend.

Within seconds, Malcolm gripped my elbow and jerked it lightheartedly, trying to get me to engage. I lay there in silence before the bed dipped. His arms cradled around my waist. The feel of his arms comforted me. His hugs were genuine. The warm breath on my neck tingled and sent various body parts steaming with excitement. Something I shouldn't enjoy. His right arm snugged me tighter. "Tell me what's wrong so I can fix it."

His kind words always consoled me whenever I was upset or overwhelmed. I knew tonight he'd get me right. I believed in this man. Not only that, but I admired him.

"I didn't think it'd end this soon," my voice cracked. "I mean...it was a dead-end relationship...but I didn't see it coming," I hinted, feeling defeated. "Another failed relationship. It's possible I'm not good at this," I suggested, complaining as Malcolm listened intently.

Malcolm interjected swiftly. "He wasn't worthy enough."

"But it was so sudden."

"There had to be signs."

"You're not making this better."

He sighed begrudgingly and gently squeezed me harder. "Take it as a sign that he wasn't the one."

"It's hard..."

"It wasn't meant to be," he repeated. "I know you're rolling your eyes."

I chuckled because he knew me so well. "And is."

"Believe me...when I say he wasn't for you. You deserve better. Repeat after me." He nudged me.

"You deserve better," I teased.

"Rory, I meant you."

"I know, silly."

"Well...say it then." He didn't raise his voice, but it was stern.

"I deserve better."

"Louder."

"I Deserve Better."

He unraveled his arm from around me and sat up, pulling me along with him. He grabbed my hand as we stood toe to toe. Lifting my chin with his finger, he nodded.

"I deserve better, and I'm going to get it," I declared with a newfound awareness.

"Better." He grinned. "With you dressed in your muumuu," he teased, flashing a sexy smile.

I released my hands from his and slapped his shoulder and cackled. "There you go playing! You know how to make me laugh through my pain."

"That's because it's our pain." He connected our hands and bored into my unsteady eyes. "When you hurt, I hurt, and vice versa."

My head jerked back, and my forehead wrinkled, taking in his words. That comment was powerful. That's why he was my best friend above all. He was my ride-or-die for life. It was so sweet how he tended to my needs before his.

Still not feeling my best, I whispered, staring at the floor. "What if I wanted to work on that relationship?"

The jerk of my hands caused me to glance up into his lopsided grin. "Aht! Aht!" He gave me the eye. "We're not stepping back, but moving forward."

I mimicked him, tilting my head from side to side.

"Well to make matters worse, your name came up in our argument."

Malcolm rolled his dark eyes. "I hate to break it to you, but he was insecure of another man. Your best friend at that."

I released my hands from his and placed them on my hips. "That's what I tried to tell him, but he wouldn't listen."

Malcolm held a smirk hidden in his eyes. "You deserve a willing partner to love you beyond your faults. Someone to help you reach your goals, teach you how to love and be loved. Someone secure in themselves to let you shine."

Okay, his words convinced me that time. They were touching as they soothed my heart and lifted my spirit.

"Thank you, Malcolm." I wrapped my arms around his waist and rested my head there for several seconds.

Malcolm was the type of man who didn't mind expressing emotions as he wrapped his around me. I could have remained in that position forever, but the words that came out of his mouth had me laughing once again.

"Okay, let's go watch an episode of '*A Different World*: *season three, episode nine 'Answered Prayers*'. That was a favorite pastime of ours. We loved watching reruns of good TV shows. Lowering my arms, I stepped out of his hug and led the way into the living room.

TWO

THE FLIGHT

Aurora

"When is the Colorado trip?"

I hurriedly jumped to my feet and placed a hand over my heart. "It's next week. Shoot!" I palmed my forehead.

"What time is your flight?"

I paced the living room, oblivious to Malcolm's question. "I don't want to fly by myself. Who can I ask last minute?" I started, mumbling names using my hands. "Dang, it's short notice too."

"Ask me."

I paused and faced him, and the crease of his mouth produced a smile on his deep, reddish brown hue.

"Malcolm, I can't ask you to do that last minute. What about your job?" I shook my head as my legs began moving again.

"What are friends for again?" His tone was light.

Pausing in my tracks, I sighed in deep thoughts. *Ask him, Aurora.* "Will you go with me, Malcolm?"

His thick eyebrows arched with a sly grin. "I mean on the trip. To Denver, Colorado. I already have a hotel and a rental car."

Standing to his gigantic height, he hovered over me. "You forgot the magic word." The crease deepened.

"Please?" I questioned with an embarrassed smile.

"Yes, silly girl. I don't know why you're tripping. It would be a mini vacay for me too."

"Thank you." I wiped the invisible sweat off of my forehead. "I didn't want to take you from your job. You know you love your job," I teased in a singsong way. Malcolm and his brother LaKeith worked in IT. He had a computer science and engineering background while LaKeith held an engineering degree.

"I'm honored to attend as your plus one." He wrapped an arm around my head in a headlock. "We got to finish this episode," he joked, walking me toward the sofa with me still in a headlock.

"Let my head go," I mocked, freeing myself from his grip. "Oh, I think I should sleep at your place Wednesday night, so we can leave on time."

The laughter from Malcolm's baritone sent a shiver down my spine. It was rich and resounding. I nudged him on the elbow. "I'm serious."

"I know you are." He shook his head shamefully. "You need to learn how to wake up like a normal person."

"I tried that and you fussed at me, remember." We got sidetracked and forgot to finish the episode, discussing my punctuality issues according to Malcolm.

"You know Atlanta airport is huge. I'm more sufficient when you're with me."

He didn't respond so I took his silence to continue. "You remember what almost happened last time," I asked with a smirk. Two years ago, we took a trip to D.C. and sure enough, we had to run through the airport because I forgot to set the alarm. It was by the grace of God we woke up 'on time' which we should have been leaving the house. The traffic wasn't too heavy at five at that particular time either.

"Yeah, I couldn't forget that." He pushed against my shoulder with his and twisted his head toward me. "Have you packed yet?"

A knowing smile he already knew. "I'm going to do it the night before so I won't forget anything."

"Yeah." He jumped to his feet and moved toward my bedroom.

"What are you doing?" I asked, getting up and following behind him. Leaning on the doorframe, I noticed him familiarizing himself with where my clothes were. He grabbed my pink luggage set from the closet. He returned to the closet and grabbed a couple of sweater dresses. I had one in every color but I was curious to see which one he'd grab. He brought out the yellow, burnt orange, and maroon dress. He lined the black and brown heeled boots beside them. He proceeded to open and close drawers, pulling out two pairs of jeans, leggings, and jeggings. Not missing the long-sleeved shirts, cardigans, and matching accessories. All of my clothes were laid out on the bed.

"Did I miss anything?" He asked confidently.

"Nope," I said, bouncing off the wall. "Thank you, smartass! I can take over from here."

"No problem."

"What time are you coming to my house on Wednesday night?"

"Six."

"Sounds good. I'll see you then."

"Alright and thank you for everything, Mal," I said, walking him to the door.

"What are friends for," he said, hugging me.

I watched him pull off into the night.

THURSDAY MORNING

Rushing as usual, we quickly hurried into the awaiting Uber and headed to the airport. Atlanta airport was busy as usual. One would think it wouldn't be at six-thirty in the morning. Sadly mistaken, it was. We retrieved our boarding passes at the Southwest terminal and handed our luggage to the Customer Service Agents. After battling the long line through TSA, a well-known line popped into my mind, 'We top flight security of the world Craig,' rushing for the boarding train. My legs were tired. Listening to Malcolm fuss at me for not picking up speed almost caused me to give him a piece of my mind. When the doors opened on the train, people rushed on. Besides being hungry and having to pee, I was also crowded, holding the metal pole. Thankfully, when it was our turn to step off, my stomach growled.

"Told you I was hungry."

"Let's go, hungry monster." He held onto my hand like a lost little child as we maneuvered through the airport.

"Wait, I got to use the bathroom first." I handed him my makeup bag and small carry-on while I held onto my purse as I proceeded to my destination. It was funny because I'd never seen someone directing traffic in the ladies' bathroom. I've been to D.C., Detroit, and Charlotte, but none like this. But it was a blessing because the employee handled the line well. It flowed with ease like a Chick-fil-A line. Exiting the bathroom, I lifted my phone and called Malcolm.

He answered swiftly. "I'm standing in front of Chick-fil-A. I got your favorite, the spicy chicken biscuit meal with O.J."

A broad grin appeared because I was thinking about the restaurant. My best friend thought of me.

"Thanks, friend, I'm on my way," I answered, heading in his direction. I spotted him standing in a tan trench coat with a pair of dark brown boots. His shoulder-length dreads were neatly twisted. His appearance from afar sparked a rumble of butterflies from my head down to my stomach. Reeling in my feelings, I lowered my gaze. My body shouldn't be responding to him. This was weird. Shaking my head to rid myself of foolery, I shivered at the thought of coming into close contact.

"Rory, you still there?" I heard him say.

"Yeah, just a few steps away." When he shifted to the left, a smile beckoned at the corner of his lips.

"Hold this while I run to the bathroom." He handed me a drink holder, a bag of good-smelling food, and my makeup bag. He placed the carry-on on the floor next to me.

I blinked, my mind somewhere else at this point.

"Rory."

My attention snapped toward him as I answered, "Sorry, I spaced out," as he took off. The men's bathroom was in front of me when he emerged from it.

"You didn't have to wait here for me, silly."

"I know, but I didn't want you looking lost like you had me a few minutes ago," I joked, playfully.

He smirked. "Whatever, come on so we can eat."

He picked up my carry-on, grabbed the drink container, and reached for the food.

"I can carry this, Mr. Power Ranger." I laughed softly, and he shook his head as we headed for the chairs, waiting for our flight. That was his nickname from me because he exuded strength and passion.

Malcolm wasted no time digging into the bag and helping himself. Before he bit his sandwich, he handed me the chicken biscuit. Another reason why he was called a Power Ranger because he took the lead and was confident enough to guide me.

After devouring Chick-fil-A food, I stretched my arms over my head as the Ramp Agent began announcing by groups.

When it was our time to load the plane, we settled in the middle toward the base of the wings. He placed the carry-on above the sectioned seat.

By allowing Malcolm to go first, he sat by the window. That was my original plan since I hated them. Placing my purse and makeup bag underneath the seats in front, I quickly straight-ened my back. Not a second later, my heart beat like a wild woman. I gripped the left armrest and closed my eyes. The plane hadn't taken off yet.

The gesture of large and warm hands comforting me partially soothed my anxiety. I mean...If I were to die, at least it'd be with my best friend.

The heavenly clouds were beautiful when I opened my eyes briefly and then closed them again. The flight took over two and a half hours to arrive in Denver, Colorado.

"Rory, we're here," I heard Malcolm's mellow tone interrupt my light sleep. "Time to get up, big head."

Blinking my eyes, I twisted my head to glance around, and sure enough, people were standing in the aisle, waiting to get off.

"You slept through the flight."

"That was my plan. You know I hate flying."

"I don't see how when you've traveled to cities before."

I reached underneath the seats to pull my bags. "That's because I had a reason to fly."

"Like now, huh?" he stated, walking behind me and grab-bing my carry-on from above.

The transportation from the airport took us to the car rental place. After adding Malcolm's name, I handed him the keys to the Nissan Rogue. Malcolm steered us from Denver to Colorado Springs where the hotel was located. We shared a room. The room had two queen-sized beds, a small refrigerator, a large TV, and a nice-sized shower with a sink on the outside. "That's weird."

"Yeah it is," he said, placing the bags on the floor. "Who thought of this brilliant idea to place the sink outside of the bathroom?"

"Right? It looks crazy. I don't know if I like this." I eyed the sink, shaking my head. "Anyways, what're we eating 'cause I'm hungry."

"Didn't you just eat?" He cocked a brow.

"That was two hours and some change ago."

"I don't know where the food goes." He walked up to me and poked my stomach. "You might have a tapeworm. You need to get that checked out." He winked.

I slapped his hand away. "Get out of my face." I spun around, dropping on top of the bed, tucking my legs underneath as I grabbed my phone.

Hearing the sound of a football game, I lifted my head to stare at him. "You're watching a football game while I'm over here starving. Mal, that ain't cool. How you gon' be my friend if you're not feeding me?" I joked.

Malcolm cut his eyes at me, picked up the white pillow, and threw it at me.

"Oh, is that what we're doing?" I teased, dropping my phone on the bed from my hand as I grabbed the pillow he threw.

"Rory, for real...you just ate. I mean...I could eat a little later."

Rolling my eyes, I muttered, "I guess we'll go later then. I do have an itinerary for the next few days. Then we have to do the meet and greet Friday night for the wedding. Saturday, you can plan something for us."

"Oh really now?" He arched his brows, and a smirk fell apart on his handsome face. "I thought you had everything planned."

"I do, but I wanted you to have a say so in what we do too." My pupils flashed with mischief.

"That sounds like a plan then."

"Thank you bestie," I expressed with an upbeat, clapping my hands.

Malcolm resumed the football game as I laid back on the bed. I scrolled through Facebook and Instagram feeds. I woke up to the sound of Malcolm's intense voice, realizing I had fallen asleep.

"Get up sleepy head. You've slept another two hours."

I sat up slowly and rubbed my eyes. "It's because you didn't let me eat yet."

The sound of his laughter rumbled my insides. It was rich and deep. "Jet lag."

"Yeah, we're like two hours ahead of time. See, it'd be four o'clock in Georgia right about now."

He sat on the edge of my bed with his phone in his hand. "What type of food are you feeling?"

"Shoot, I could go for a burger or a sandwich."

"Out of all the things you could possibly eat, you name a burger and sandwich."

I shrugged. "Well, what do you suggest?"

His eyes spoke as they became more focused. His gaze intensified, giving off an almost smoldering effect at the corners. The awkward silence persisted for a while until he finally coughed, breaking the tension.

"American is fine. I'll look at the reviews, and then I'll send you the link."

"Okay," was all I could mutter at the time.

We ended at an upscale western-like restaurant with high ceilings, retro, industrial pendant lighting, wine barrels, and wooden bar stools and booths.

Malcolm ordered a Long Island Iced Tea and water, and I ordered their Blue Lagoon. It was served in a highball glass. The fruitiness of the drink did its justice. I didn't feel it until after my third one.

A natural tan Asian waitress with bright Auburn shoulder-length hair and green eyes took our order. The food didn't take long to be brought out to us. I will admit we were the only people of color in the restaurant. I didn't mind. I just took notice. I glanced down at the Cuban sandwich and hot fries. I wiggled in my seat. I couldn't wait to dig the fries into the ketchup and mustard mix.

"So have you met the woman your cousin is marrying on Sunday?" Malcolm asked, cutting his steak into bite-size pieces.

"From a group picture my aunt shared with the family."

"So you haven't met her personally?"

"No, it'll be my first time on Sunday." Biting the sandwich, I moaned sarcastically, swaying back and forth. I reached for a napkin to wipe my mouth. "It's going to be a first for the family."

"What do you mean?" he asked mid-sentence.

"Her family is from Nepal."

Malcolm stopped chewing. "She's Hindu?"

I shrugged. "Her religion...I don't know but he loves her and that's good for me."

THREE
THE RESTAURANT

Aurora

As the conversation dwindled from my cousin's upcoming wedding, it steered to what was next on the agenda for the evening. As I pondered, I whipped out my phone but forgot the rule.

"You're paying?" Malcom grinned as he chugged down his drink.

"Shoot, I forgot." I laid the phone on the tabletop. "I was looking up something for us to do before the night was over."

"It's only three thirty."

"That's beside the point." I stuck out my tongue.

"What about the meet and greet tonight?"

"That's tomorrow night."

"I knew that," he laughed.

"But I was thinking maybe go explore some stores and sceneries."

"You're not adding more to the three bags you brought."

My head twisted sideways. "I know that. I want to see if

they sell different items than the ones back home." I retrieved my phone, searching for nearby clothing shops. "There's a Ross and TJ Maxx."

Malcolm picked up his ice water and put it to his lips when my phone beeped. I stared at the text.

Marshon: Just checking to see how you were doing?

I sighed deeply and unexpectedly rolled my eyes.

"Your ex?" he accused, setting the glass on the table and piercing me with those dark eyes.

"Yeah, but I'm not going to answer it."

"Why not?"

As I looked up from my phone, his stoic expression was tense, revealing no emotion behind his gaze.

"I don't want to get upset again, which I already feel my pressure going up."

He licked his thick lips as the words flowed. "Don't allow someone who's insignificant to ruin your happiness."

I never said I was happy. Because I gave the impression that I was fine, Malcolm assumed I was okay.

"Easier said than done," I replied, ignoring the text and placing it flat down.

MALCOLM RAISED his hand to signal the waitress and asked for another drink. The tension between the text message and my response of not replying to it expanded. I shifted my gaze around the restaurant. Changing the subject to a safer topic, I stated, "Don't act like you don't like window shopping."

The corner of Malcolm's eyes crinkled. The waitress placed his drink in front. He picked it up and stared at me intensely.

It was hot in here suddenly. Picking up the ice water, I gulp heavily.

"Of course, I like to window shop," he stated, sipping the Long Island.

While in college, our funds were low, but when we got paid. We headed to the stores and bought the items if they weren't sold out already.

Malcolm finished his drink and paid for lunch. The majority of the stores were within distance of each other. Of course, we had to stop and grab coffee from Dunkin. I preferred a sweeter concoction. I got my regular caramel latte with extra cream and drizzle, and Malcolm chose differently by ordering a pumpkin spice latte. I swore up and down caramel was all I needed until he let me try his. I was surprised. It didn't taste that differently from caramel. The only difference I could taste was the cinnamon and lots of it. With more energy in our system, Malcom drove around the city, stopping at the stores I mentioned earlier along with others.

The people in the city were friendly, complimenting me on my hair. The color intrigued them, I presume. Not only were the people nice, but it was the atmosphere. Atlanta was loud and busy like the people who lived there but not here. It was calm and quiet in Colorado Springs. The area seemed expensive, and the buildings had unique architectural designs. There weren't many of us, but there were other people of color like Indians, not the Natives but the other ones and Mexicans.

Driving through the city, I spotted a peculiar building. I knew it was some kind of hospital, but as people held a pump to their car, I was shocked it was a gas station. Even the convenience stores were shaped differently from ours back home. If I had to describe Colorado Springs in a few words, I'd say it's tranquil, serene, expansive, and distinctive. In all my years, I've never encountered such kind and friendly people. I just wanted to take some of them back home to Georgia.

FOUR
MEET & GREET

Malcolm

S ince I picked out Aurora's clothes before the trip, I told
her she could pick out my clothes for the gathering tonight
for the meet and greet. She studied me for the longest time.

"Are you serious?"

"Yeah," I answered, relaxing against the sofa and watching
another football game but on mute. Usher music played in the
background on speakers.

"Well...you ain't got to tell me but once," she agreed,
walking toward my heavy-duty gray suitcase. She dragged it
and struggled to lift it.

Letting out a groan, I jumped to my feet to assist her. "Why
didn't you ask me to get it?"

She rolled her eyes and flicked her wrist. "Because I can
do it."

I threw my hands up and stepped back, shaking my head.
Aurora was a determined woman.

She unzipped the suitcase and unraveled many of the

folded clothing I neatly set apart. She laid a pair of black socks to the side and dark denim with a fitted tan cashmere sweater with a black dress shirt. Setting aside my favorite tan Oxfords, she tossed my trench coat to the side to complete my look for the evening.

"You like," she asked, angling her head and waiting for my approval. I had to admit she knew what I liked. I approved.

"Yep." I gave her a thumbs up.

Aurora grabbed her clothing and stepped into the bathroom. As she washed her body, I turned the TV to face me as I sat on the edge of the bed. When the door opened, we locked eyes. I grabbed my underwear and socks and did the same thing.

Stepping out of the bathroom, I ran into Aurora as she put on her right eyelash. "My bad...didn't know you'd be in my way." I winked, grabbing the towel snugly.

"Yeah, right!" She smirked, moving closer to the mirror. "You're trying to mess up my look so I won't get a man tonight."

My face hardened. Lips pressed together, eyes firm, and nostrils flared. As a friend, I didn't want to hear anything about another man with her. Deep down inside, I knew she was hurting from her break-up. I hoped that my being here would solve the sadness and restore happiness back into her life.

I walked past her, grabbed my clothes, and strolled back into the bathroom. As I stepped out, I noticed her beauty immediately. Her burgundy-red twistout took on an editorial appeal. She recently got an asymmetrical cut with more hair on one side. The yellow bodycon dress tailored her size twelve curviness well. The color complimented her skin tone. The dress material was stretchy and sheer, accentuating its texture. She paired it with black pumps and canary hoop earrings.

Aurora's fashion sense was runway-worthy. I was without words. I knew my girl could dress, but she blew me away.

"Cat got your tongue." She pursed her lips.

My pupils lowered to the floor as I dusted off my pants, anything to distract my dirty thoughts from going in the gutter for my friend.

"Ready?" Her eyes sparkled.

I nodded, picking up my coat while she grabbed her double-breasted belted overcoat lying over the arm of the sofa.

I'm not saying anything different from what I know. Aurora was the type when she walked into a room, all eyes fell on her. But it was me who walked into the common area. She had that effect on me.

We arrived at this sophisticated restaurant. The upstairs area was reserved for the meet and greet. As we climbed up the stairs, we could hear soft instrumental music being played through hidden speakers. I could feel the melody resonating with me, making the social atmosphere even more pleasant.

Waiters and waitresses were roaming around taking drink orders and passing out drinks.

"Ooh, this is nice," Aurora chimed as she moved in front of me.

I agreed with a nod. People were coming and going in different directions. The space was intimate but spacious enough to host up to seventy people. It was a habit of mine to place a hand on her lower back.

"It's warm in here," she muttered, flapping the neck of the modern coat.

I leaned forward into her ear. "You're going through the changes."

She popped me on the shoulder, and soon a woman toward the back of the room waved. The attractive woman sported a black crochet jumpsuit as she strutted toward us.

"That's my favorite cousin!" Aurora beamed, the corners of her eyes smizing. She waved her hand and summoned her cousin to come with a flick of her wrist.

"Cousin," the woman screamed and hugged Aurora around the neck. "How was the flight?"

"The same. You know I be ready to get off as soon as I get on." The sound of Aurora's laughter was whimsical over the noise in the venue.

The moment the woman twisted her head toward me, I inhaled a deep breath.

"Um, who is this?" she inquired, scanning me from the top of my twisted dreads and down to my outfit, not missing a beat as she winked.

Aurora flicked her hair. "Girl, this is Mal."

"Mal?"

I nodded, flashing a smile.

"Ohh!" She dipped her head back, side-eyeing Aurora. Her broad smile widened, facing me. "---This is Malcolm," she pressed her glossy red lips together. "It's nice to finally meet you. Rory talks about you all the time." Eyeing Aurora again, she bit her lip.

Aurora shook her head embarrassingly and stepped closer to me, placing her hand over my forearm. "Yes, this is the bestie."

"I see why." She pursed her lips upward. "Welcome to the family," she yelled over the noise with outstretched arms.

Being respectful of Aurora's family, I swiftly returned the gesture.

"So, Charlotte, what have you been up to?"

"Girl, nothing too much." She flipped her wrist, gripping Aurora's arm in hers, and looked toward the stairs. "Where's Shon, is he coming?"

I almost knew every body language of Aurora's. I knew at the moment she was embarrassed as her back stiffened. Trying not to be noticeable, she faked a smile. She turned Charlotte away and tried whispering low, but I overheard her when she said, 'We're not together anymore. He broke up with me.'

"Dang girl," Charlotte commented, glancing over her shoulder. "You know he was never good enough for you."

My gaze intensified when Aurora locked eyes with mine. "That's the same thing Mal said."

Charlotte released Aurora's arm and stood next to me. "I'm glad we're on the same page."

"That's what besties are for."

Charlotte's infectious smile widened as she glanced suspiciously between Aurora and me. "You know what they say, right?"

"What they say?"

"To get over someone, you need to get under someone new." Charlotte's laugh was husky.

Her comment irked me. Again, I didn't want to hear Aurora with another man. Sooner than later, Aurora introduced me to other family members I'd never met. She conjugated with her family that was in attendance as we sat down at a table and indulged in alcohol. Charlotte questioned why her parents didn't come, and she told her step-father couldn't get off from his job, so her mother agreed to stay home and miss the wedding.

Charlotte kept glancing in my direction all night. I didn't want to pursue anything with her because she was Aurora's cousin. For Aurora to say they were close, I couldn't do that. Although Charlotte was attractive, she was Aurora's best cousin. I was not about keeping it in the family. Charlotte was the same height as Aurora, standing at five seven even. Her skin possessed a natural golden tone. Her eyes were low, possibly from the alcohol she'd been consuming.

"Mal, I'm going to mingle," Aurora announced with a tilt of her head.

Cutting my eyes and raising a brow, I bowed my head.

"You're going to be okay, right?" She reached across the table and laid hers on top of my hand.

Gaze lowering to her hand, my heart warmed. She cared about my feelings. "I'm good. Go do you."

Returning a sincere gesture, she slid from the table, dusted off her dress, and walked away.

The cousin who was getting married, finally graced us with his commanding presence with his fiancé. Her family was in attendance as well.

FIVE
NEW CHIC

Malcolm

While sipping on my choice of liquor, I realized Aurora had been gone a minute now. I searched for her among the scenery, even though I knew she was safe with her cousin. I didn't see her, so I got up in search of her. As I rounded the corner, a gorgeous brown-skinned woman stopped me and started a conversation.

"Hi, I'm Cassandra," she whispered. "I've been watching you all night." She held out her hand.

Women were brave nowadays. I didn't find it a turn-off. It did the opposite and intrigued me.

"Are you going to stare at my hand or shake it?" she asked, batting her eyelashes and holding a drink in her other hand.

Sheepishly, I shook her hand and leaned down. "I'm sorry, I'm Malcolm by the way."

"No problem." She slipped her hand from mine. "What are you drinking on?"

"Rum and Coke."

ing, but I didn't want her sad and depressed about her
situation.

"Maybe you're looking in the wrong direction," I suggested.

The corner of her mouth lifted. We engaged in small talk as
we headed toward the snack table. I grabbed some meatballs,
bite-size tandoori chicken, and chunks of watermelon. Finished
with the finger food, I threw the plate away and finished my
drink.

"Thanks for keeping me company, but you seem eager to
get to your friend. If you ever need your lap warm tonight, I'm
down." She winked, reaching her free hand up to my face.

I caught her hand and kissed the inside before searching for
Aurora.

Aurora was sitting at the back, away from the crowd, deep
in conversation with a dark-skin and bald-headed man. I
spotted her and made my way towards her, my heart beating
faster with each step. Aurora had her long legs crossed as she
sat forward with a drink in her hand. I knew she could hold her
drink, but I wasn't sure how many she already had. She'd been
drinking all night, starting with an espresso martini at our table
earlier, and now sipping on a fruity drink. As I approached
them, their conversation came to a halt. Politely excusing
myself, I turned to Aurora and asked if she was ready to leave. I
couldn't tell what her expression was as she answered.

. . .

"ACTUALLY," she started, waving her hand outward. "Camden and I are going out after we leave here."

The answer she gave me surprised me. I wasn't expecting that. Masking my disappointment, I leaned over and whispered, "We rode together. We leave together."

Aurora rolled her eyes. "Can I talk to you for a moment?" She turned to Camden and smiled. "I won't be long."

He nodded, picking up his drink and stepping away.

"Mal, I appreciate you, but I'm going with Camden."

"You don't know him."

"I know that."

"What if?"

"No." She placed her hand on my chest. "I know where I am and what I'm doing. If I need you, I'll call you. Can you give me that?"

I didn't want to agree, but I had no choice. She was going to do as she pleased. "Just be careful."

"Always," she stated, turning to find Camden standing with two other men.

I pivoted and found myself at the bar ordering another drink. This time, whiskey on the rocks.

I felt a poke on my shoulder. Cassandra pulled out a stool and planted herself next to me. "I'm still down if you are."

"We can go to your place or a hotel." What I agreed to do, I wouldn't do it at the hotel I shared with Aurora.

"We can go to mine. Follow me," she stated, her chocolate eyes flashing lust.

I drowned the rest of my drink and closed out my tab, watching Aurora grab her coat from the booth before heading downstairs.

Cassandra lived twenty minutes away from the restaurant. It was nice as I stepped over the threshold and into her home.

She hung up her coat and removed her shoes. "Would you like something to drink?" she asked over her shoulder.

"Water is fine."

"Suit yourself." She opened her refrigerator and handed me a bottle of water. "I'm going to freshen up."

"Take your time." I removed my shoes and placed them by the door. I set my coat along the back of a chair. I made myself as comfortable as I could be sitting on her plush sofa.

As I sat there, thoughts of Aurora kept surfacing in my mind. However, the sound of Cassandra's footsteps abruptly interrupted my thoughts. She stopped suddenly and twirled around, enticing me. She was no longer in the sequin cocktail dress but a sleeveless floral slip.

"Are you ready to be amazed?" she purred, picking up the remote and turning on soft music.

She eased her way toward me and straddled my lap. She kissed me with a need, touching my chest and holding my head. I closed my eyes and felt my sweater going over my head. The buttons came next. Cassandra didn't get farther than she planned due to me grabbing a hold of her hands.

"What's wrong," she groaned deeply, rocking back and forth.

"I can't do this. Not to myself," I mumbled coherently. Grasping Cassandra around the waist, I held her in place and pierced her gaze. "You're a beautiful woman. But, I'm just not the man for you."

"What? I don't understand!"

"You won't. I'm sorry I wasted your time."

Lips pressed together, she climbed off my lap and folded her arms under her breast.

Jumping to my feet, I threw the sweater over my half-button shirt and shrugged into my coat, slipping into my shoes. "Have a good night, Cassandra." Without looking back, I rushed to the rental car and cruised toward the hotel.

Entering the hotel, my stomach dropped when I didn't see Aurora in her bed. Kicking off my shoes and hanging my coat in the closet, I lay against the bed.

The sun blazed brightly through the curtains. I shifted in bed. Hearing the door open, I turned toward it and saw Aurora coming in. She looked disheveled.

"Good afternoon, sleepy head." She smiled, peeling off her clothes and grabbing fresh ones, entering the bathroom.

AFTERNOON? I rolled over and reached for my phone. It was 12:05. I slept through the morning, and that wasn't me. Usually, I was an early riser. My stomach flip-flopped. I felt nauseous. I clenched my stomach and hoped it helped. It didn't. Leaning forward, I realized my jeans were still on. I knew I was losing it because I never slept in them. That was something I didn't do was sleep in my day clothes.

Aurora exited the bathroom fully dressed in jeans and a sweater, makeup-free. "Hey, let's get moving because there's so much to do today. I want to explore the city."

Forcing a smile, I slid out of bed and entered the bathroom. Nothing came up. Somehow, I didn't feel like myself. It started when Aurora walked in this morning wearing a satisfied smirk on her face. Gritting my teeth, I rubbed a hand down my face.

I had to figure out why I was feeling like this. I knew it had to do with Aurora. Opening the door and moving sluggishly, I grabbed my clothing from the suitcase and laid them on the bed. It felt like I stayed in the shower for a long time, and then the knocking and shouting through the door confirmed it.

"Let's go sleepyhead. I see you had a good time last night. You can't get up," Aurora yelled on the other side of the door.

Shaking my head, I rinsed off and stepped out, dry toweling. I opened the door, and she seemed occupied with the TV while I took care of my personal hygiene.

"How did it go last night?"

"Fine."

"You okay?"

"Yeah," I voiced, grabbing my clothes and entering the bathroom.

Fully dressed, my gaze connected with Aurora's. Her smile illustrated the satisfaction on her oval-shaped face. "You want to know about my night."

Truthfully, I wanted Aurora to keep her adventure to herself, but she'd know something was up with me. "Sure," I lied, grabbing my coat from the closet.

"After we got back to his home, he couldn't wait to get his hands on me. He rushed me to his bedroom. Between taking off the clothes---" I held my hand in the air.

"I get it. You had a good time. Let's go explore what Colorado has to offer."

Aurora wasn't happy I cut her off mid-sentence by twisting up her nose. She should understand I didn't want to hear about her sexcapade.

"I don't know why you're hating. It seems like you had a good time as well," she sassed, snatching her coat from the chair as she followed behind me into the hallway.

Aurora pulled out her phone and suggested going to explore a cave. It was an hour away. The ride was semi-quiet except for the music in the background. Mountains upon mountains were in plain view. Yahweh's creation was astonishing to examine while driving. Of course, Aurora snapped pictures and recorded them as well. Amid the mountains was an aircraft. Odd, but logical when the Air Force Academy was nearby.

Aurora didn't realize the caves were in the mountains until I turned the curve. Her eyes got big, and then she shut them rapidly. The next thing I knew, Aurora grasped the handle above the door. Her body turned inward as she crouched, covering her knees.

"Look at how high we are," I teased as we rounded the sharp left turn.

"No!" she quietly uttered.

"You booked the tickets." I roared in laughter.

"I didn't realize it was in a mountain."

"You're silly, Rory. Where did you think the cave was?"

"Not in a mountain. Go real slow around these curves." She warned viciously.

"I am," I argued, making it safely to the top of the mountain.

Cave of the Winds had a shopping center. We explored the center and waited for our guided tour.

Our group of about 15 people followed the female tour guide as she led us into the cave entrance. The tour guide told a story as we walked, ducked through small openings, zipped through narrow paths, and climbed millions of stairs; it felt like all the while appreciating the cave itself. The feeling was exhilarating.

After safely returning to the road, Aurora tried to book tickets for the Broadmoor Manitou train ride, but the tickets were sold out for the day. We settled on a scenic steam train ride exploring the area's gold mining history at Cripple Creek.

Aurora was starving, so we stopped at a local restaurant to eat. Many of these restaurants were Mexican-based, but we didn't mind. Food was food when you're hungry. Since I was with my friend, my anger dissipated by the evening. During the ride back to the hotel, Aurora got a call from her cousin to go hang out.

"Hold on, let me ask." She put her phone on mute and asked me, "Charlotte wants to know if you want to hang out with us later tonight?"

"We can."

She unmuted the phone and continued her conversation with Charlotte. They talked all the way back to the hotel.

The night actually turned out nice. Charlotte kept Aurora and me company with drinks, music, and snacks at a friend's house party. Aurora mingled with her other family members in attendance. When she moved out of my peripheral view, she sent me a text.

Rory: You good?

Me: Yeah, I'm good. Enjoy yourself.

Rory: You sure because the last time I enjoyed myself, you got an attitude. And I can't have my friend mad at me for enjoying myself.

I stared at the text, holding a cup of Hennessy and smiling at myself for tripping.

Me: I'm sorry, I didn't want you tripping about ol' boy.

Rory: I promise you, I'm good.

Me: Noted. Have fun, and I'm ready when you are.

"Texting the bestie."

My mouth tensed as I gripped the cup tightly. I swung my gaze down into speculating, brown eyes.

The smirk reappeared. "I would think you two have something going on." She glanced in Aurora's direction. "Would you say I'm right?"

"Eyes see what they want to see." I downed the rest of the alcohol as she pierced me with a knowing look. "We're just friends."

"We'll see." She left where I was standing.

Later that night, Aurora and I talked well into the night across from one another after she yawned a couple of times.

"Go to bed, sleepy head."

"I will if you keep talking."

Shaking my head, I turned off the TV. "You'd sleep better if you didn't snore."

"I don't snore," she argued.

SIX

THE WEDDING

Aurora

Today was the day we scrambled around, knowing we knew the time to be there, but once again, Malcolm was waiting for me to finish the final touches on my makeup as he waited patiently on the sofa. "I'm ready," I confessed, grabbing my coat.

Standing up from the sofa, he opened the door with a smile.

Once we got to the location of the wedding, it was another architectural design. When I stepped out of the car, the partial sun fell just right on Malcolm, making me second-guess my decision. He was looking so damn good. Like he took my breath away. I fanned myself and asked, *Who was this guy? Was he single?*

He reached between us and grabbed my hand. "What's on your mind?"

"Nothing," I lied, glancing around. "I'm just taking in the beauty of nature."

The wedding colors were rustic brown, champagne, and

olive green throughout the venue. We were told there was free alcohol until nine tonight.

The bridal party mismatched sexy and satin, off-shoulder, olive-green dresses, and the groomsmen dressed in rustic brown suits. They looked superb. The wedding progressed with my cousin dressed in a two-piece, champagne-colored suit vest and jacket and rustic brown trousers, complemented by a matching tie.

In anticipation of his bride-to-be, my cousin waited next to the preacher with a smile shining brighter than the sun. In my heart, I felt he loved her very much. When his hand reached his eyes, I witnessed him rubbing it back and forth. My cousin was shedding tears. I pressed a hand to my heart and tapped Malcolm on the leg, pointing my finger and whispering, "He's crying."

The best was yet to come when the bride stunned us in a champagne mermaid bridal gown.

The wedding ceremony was captivating. The photographer snapped pictures at the wedding party while the rest of the guests entered the venue, some at the bar and others socializing inside. Malcolm stepped away to the bathroom while I stood in line at the bar. Pulling my phone from my purse, I noticed a text from my ex.

Marshon: Why haven't you returned my calls or texts?

I stared at the question. Did Marshon have amnesia or something? It was like he knew when to mess me up in the head.

Me: You broke up with me. Why would I call you?

Marshon: I was thinking about us. You.

Me: Well, I wish you the best.

Marshon: Can I see you this weekend?

Me: For what?

Marshon: I'm going to be the man you want me to be. Admit my feelings. I miss you.

I started to reply.

"Everything okay?" Malcolm's deep baritone near my ear caused me to flinch. I spun around, fumbling my phone as I tucked it away in my hand-held purse. "Yeah," I stuttered. "What's your first drink?"

His brows lowered at my purse. I fidgeted under his stare. His head lifted and connected with mine, pulling a smile from me. "Long Island."

I flicked my wrist. "Blah...try something new for a change. Let me order you a drink."

"Go ahead." He moved behind me and placed a hand on my lower back. With his touch, I almost jumped out of my skin. Butterflies ripped from the top of my head to my stomach as shivers raced down my spine. For some reason, I wasn't feeling right. Maybe it was hot, but whatever it was, I needed a drink fast.

The bartender behind the counter smiled and asked, "What can I get for you?"

"Yes, let me get an Amaretto Sour and Mai Tai."

The bartender swiftly made the drinks two at a time, showing off her skills as she flipped the bottle and twirled them around her back.

A couple of surrounding people and myself gave her a standing ovation. I thanked the bartender and passed the Mai Tai to Malcolm.

Malcolm bobbed his head and brought the drink up to his lips. His mouth was perfectly sculpted. Medium-sized lips with a tiny peach fuzz under the chin. When his goatee was longer, I used to run my fingers through it. He claimed he got tired of me messing up his beard, so he cut it off. Back to his lips, they were captivating. I was mesmerized by the shape of them. I couldn't take my eyes off him.

"Let's go mingle," he suggested, and I nodded, quickly placing the clear cup to my lips.

"Cuff It Remix" blared from the speakers, and we crossed the room to my cousins, aunts, and uncles. We talked about the wedding until it was time for the seating for dinner. Once seated, we waited until the hostess called for each table to fix their food. I sat beside Charlotte at the table with our twin guy cousins, Dante and his girlfriend, Stacy, Daniel and his wife, Brittany, and Catrice, our other cousin. Malcolm sat beside me as my plus one.

Charlotte elbowed me. "So, what's up with you and him." She nodded her head at Malcolm.

Leaning toward her side and away from Malcolm's ears, I uttered, "I keep telling you we're best friends and nothing more."

"Have y'all tried being more than friends and something didn't go right?"

"No," I whispered. Malcolm faced me with a raised brow, and I returned the gesture.

"Table six," the announcer said into the microphone.

"Let's go eat," I stated, trying to end the conversation as we headed toward the dining hall.

"You're not running from this conversation, Rory. I've seen the way he looks at you. And you...him."

"Charlotte, do you know you see too much?"

"I've been told."

We laughed as we began the assembly line behind others. Malcolm went one way and Charlotte and I the other.

"But you ain't curious though?"

"No," I lied.

"Girl, I'm trying to tell you. Y'all are more than friends. If not, y'all will be soon. I wish my best friend was my man so I wouldn't have to worry about getting to know him."

I stopped and gazed at her. "Isn't your best friend, Renee?"

She smirked, hitting me on the arm. "I'm talking about if I had a male best friend, heffa!"

I laughed at her. I knew what she meant, but I had to mess with her.

We walked back toward our table with our plates in our hands. Charlotte tilted her head at an angle towards me. "I bet he won't leave you alone to dance by yourself too long."

Denying the truth was getting harder each day.

"Want to bet?"

"We're friends," I stressed, sliding into my seat. After saying grace, I lifted my eyes and spotted a reddish-brown hue among the faces in the crowd. His physical stature was muscular with a lean cut, his dreads neatly styled. He was stylish in a navy two-piece suit. Malcolm styled it with a black dress shirt underneath and chestnut Oxfords on his feet. My face burned with a passion that I couldn't have. I hated the growing attraction I had for him. How could I? He was my best friend. To help fight these feelings, I abruptly stood and dashed toward the bar.

The Reception

My eyes skimmed the dance floor, searching for my friend as I bobbed my head along with the "Shake Sumn." The DJ dropped a mix of club bangers. Sipping cranberry vodka had me almost moving onto the dance floor, but I held my cool on the sideline and watched everyone else. People were bouncing and jumping up and down in a circle. The dance floor was hyped.

Aurora danced with Charlotte in a corner of the dance floor, holding a different drink. I couldn't tell what she was sipping on from a distance, but she was lit, swaying her head from side to side. She was vibing to the beat. I watched her all night, giving her space as she mingled and laughed with the wedding party and her family. It was time for me to make my way to her side of the floor, except I didn't have a chance when Cassandra stepped in front of me.

She placed a hand against my chest and shouted, "No hard feelings." Her lids lifted seductively. My gaze shifted away from Aurora and lowered to her breast.

Bouncing my head to the beat of "Blow the Whistle" while holding my liquor, Cassandra's hand lowered and encircled my waist and rocked with me.

We danced to a few more songs together when Chris Brown serenaded the speakers. As the song ended, my cup was empty. "Do you want a drink?"

"Yes," she acknowledged, following me to the bar.

Standing to the side, it was a habit of mine as I placed my hand on the lower part of women's backs.

She peeked over her shoulder and smiled at me. Returning to the bartender, she said, "Can I get a lemon drop?"

The bartender nodded, mixing vodka, triple sec, simple syrup, and a fresh drop of lemon juice.

"Surprise to see me, huh?"

I leaned down because I didn't quite hear her. "What you say?"

"I said," she raised her voice over the loud music. "Surprise to see me?"

"Yeah...kinda. I thought you'd risk avoiding me."

"Well, I play hard to get when I want something or someone." She winked, moving the cup to her lush lips.

A smirk slipped from the corner of my mouth.

My gaze found its way onto Aurora's twerking to a mutual song we both liked. Charlotte wasn't far behind her as she and Aurora battled a twerk session.

"Is that her?"

My gaze shot straight to Cassandra.

"I see the way you look at her." She finished her drink. "Wait, isn't that your friend?"

I turned up the drink, and before I knew it, I headed back

to the bar. Grabbing a jack and coke, I pivoted. Cassandra held a smirk on her face as I walked past her.

"Malcolm." I hated I heard my name. I stopped and turned around to face her.

"You're in love with your best friend."

My posture stiffened.

She stepped closer, pulled on my arm, and smiled crookedly. The smile broadened bright as hell. "Does she know?"

I rolled my eyes as she assumed. "Nice talking to you, Cassandra, but I got to go." Giving her two fingers, I strolled toward Aurora. No one knew anything about my feelings for Aurora. It was crazy to feel this way about her in the first place. I tried wrestling with my thoughts and feelings, but in the end, she won.

The DJ started playing some Indian music for the bride's family. Some people sat out and bobbed their heads while her family continued to bounce around on the song. When the DJ played "Back That Thang Up," Aurora left the dance floor to find me. She jerked my hand and yelled, "This our jam!"

I passed someone my empty cup. Aurora wasted no time twerking against me. Amid the gripping and gyrating, the crowd hyped us up. We tuned everyone out as I danced with my friend.

The song ended shortly with another snappy tempo, "Shoulder Lean." Aurora and I locked eyes on a deeper level as she started throwing her hands in the air, bouncing toward me. "The DJ playing our songs tonight," she shouted over the ear-splitting music.

Back in college, we made this our anthem song. It was so crazy that we created a routine for this song. Anytime it came on the radio, whether it was at my dorm, hers, or a friend's, we'd break out with the dance. My shoulders leaned into the rhythm. Aurora was my hyped man as she crossed the floor, leaning and bouncing her shoulders until she was right under me. We swayed together, her hip onto mine. Resting my arm on her lower back, we bobbed and tilted, rocking back and forth as the crowd chanted, "Go Rory. Go Rory....aye!"

At this moment, it felt just like college. My girl and I having fun dancing like always without any cares or worries. Just having a good time.

The DJ did an abrupt switch as he announced, "I'm slowing it down for the lovers out there." He played, "I Want to be Your Man."

The movie, 'Love and Basketball' popped into my mind as this slow jam vibrated in my ears. Aurora wrapped her arms around my neck. I placed my arms around and locked my hands on her lower back as we rocked from side to side. "I Want to be Your Man," was the vibe in this moment.

I could smell the alcohol from her breath and mine. This night was epic for both of us. I wondered if that was her ex texting her when I popped up on her earlier. I didn't get him. He dumped her but was missing her. Yeah, he messed up a good thing. And he won't get her back if I have a say so.

"What?"

I cut my eyes at my friend, shaking my head. "I didn't say anything."

"Oh, I heard you mumble."

My forehead lowered onto hers as we swayed to the rhythm.

"This feels so good. Me and you."

Was she saying what I hoped she was saying? Nah, I knew she'd been drinking tonight and wouldn't take advantage of her vulnerable state. I ignored her mumblings.

Aurora was enjoying the feel of my skin as she ran her fingers along the base of my neck. Her soft skin massaged me as I gazed at the top of her hair. Unlocking her hands from the tight grip, her hands moved forward and caressed my earlobes in a circular pattern. Lifting her neck, she stared with hungry eyes through heavy lids.

My breath caught in my throat, staring at my best friend. Knots bubbled in my stomach. It wasn't gas but nervousness. I stared longingly, waiting.

Her eyes seemed to twinkle under the flashing lights above us.

She grasped my neck again, pulling my head down. Her lips were soft against mine. She whimpered against my lips, moaning my name.

"Uh um." Charlotte cleared her throat with her hand, eyeing us.

Pulling my head back and glancing around, they connected to Charlotte standing on my right.

Charlotte pursed her lips knowingly, eyes rolling as she held a drink.

"We should go," I mumbled against her lips.

Her eyes jutted open and gave a shaky smile. "I'm not ready yet."

"Okay, a few more songs."

She stepped back and continued to dance, not missing a beat.

I left the floor and strolled to the bathroom to relieve myself. When I stepped out, Cassandra posted on the wall.

"I guess you've been waiting for that a while. And I hope she's everything you've been looking for. It was good meeting you, Malcolm. And remember if she doesn't work for you, you can always call me." Cassandra slipped her number in my hand and strutted out of the building.

Chasing one woman while the other one chased me.

It was ten when we left the venue. I was sober enough to drive us safely to the hotel. I looked to my left, and Aurora was calling hawgs. Easing into the hotel room, I pulled off her shoes and coat. I flipped back the covers and tucked Aurora under the covers. I discarded my wedding attire and entered the bath-room to relieve myself again. I tiptoed to the bed and jumped under the covers. Tomorrow's flight was early.

Sometime during the night, I felt the bed dip. It was Aurora. She was kissing my neck and whispering, '*I miss us*'.'

My nostril flared, inhaling deeply. "Rory," I moaned, my length hardening inside my pajamas.

"I want you... to kiss me---" she panted seductively. "---As if...you won't... leave me." Her voice whimpered, fisting my shirt.

The realization hit hard. Aurora missed her ex. It wasn't me she wanted, but him.

SEVEN

AWKWARDNESS

Aurora

I remembered everything last night. My cheeks were on fire from the embarrassment. My thoughts were jumbled. I lusted after my best friend. How many drinks did I consume to have the courage to do so? Snatching my clothes and stuffing them into my luggage had me going off for no reason. I wasn't mad at Malcolm but myself. I crossed the ultimate line by kissing him. "Ugh!" I sighed disgustingly.

Malcolm glanced at me with a puzzled expression, forehead wrinkled and nose scrunched. "You okay?"

"Yeah." I waved my hand dismissively, squatting down. "Just packing before we leave in an hour."

Malcolm was punctual as we boarded the plane. The flight itself was tense between us. Despite our lack of conversation, he did share with me the upcoming activities we planned before coming on this trip. He also invited me to a breast cancer function toward the end of October. Forcing a smile, I told him

I'd try to come, but in reality, I was embarrassed to show my face. What would he think of me?

The Uber ride back at Malcolm's was worse. The Uber driver didn't play music as he soared to our destination. Exiting the van, I swiftly strolled toward my car and placed my luggage there. Usually, I lingered at Malcolm's place, but not today. Lying through my teeth, I volunteered information. "Since I'm running off a few hours of sleep, I'm going to head home and get some much-needed rest." I waved, closing the trunk and sliding behind the wheel of my Honda Insight.

Malcolm nodded, dragging his luggage toward the front door. He stopped and stared at me as if he wanted to question my sanity. He waved quickly. I didn't waste time backing out of his driveway. Once home, I showered and rested on the sofa, flipping through the TV channels. Nothing was entertaining to me. I couldn't wrap my mind around what happened in Colorado. Geesh, I hated what I did. Now, we were going to be awkward around each other this weekend. I could cancel on him and tell him I got a stomach bug. Or maybe, go to my parents' house and spend the night so he won't come look for me. My mother would accuse me of hiding or running away from someone, which was partially accurate. But why did I make a pass at Malcolm? *Maybe it's because of your breakup? Yeah, that's it.* Although I was having a conversation with myself, I needed answers. I dialed Charlotte's number.

"Hey cousin, are you just getting in?"

"Yeah, we got in a while ago, but I'm at home."

"Where's Malcolm?"

"At home."

She blew out a deep sigh. "Now, you know as well as I do that y'all have a thing for each other."

I didn't respond to her shenanigans.

"Sunday night told it all. You're in love with him," she squealed in my ears.

"I can't be," I protested. "He's my best friend."

"And best friends make the best lovers."

I palmed my forehead. "I can't. He's genuinely just my friend. And I will admit---" I lifted my hand in agreement. "---I...I took it too far at the reception." I lowered my head, not like she could see me. "The atmosphere was lit. And the drinks were coming," I exclaimed, trying to convince myself that's all it was.

"And your body was horny." She burst into an uncontrollable fit of laughter, snorting in the process.

"Charley!" My nickname for her when she got on my nerves.

"Rory!"

"I know you're fighting this tooth and nail, but you're in love with your bestie," she teased. "I know you need to sort out your mixed feelings. New topic, but what're you doing this weekend?" Charlotte shifted subjects like panties.

Groaning and rolling my eyes, I answered cautiously, "Malcolm and I have fall activities this weekend."

"Proves my point," she sassed, smacking her lips.

"We've already made the plans. I thought about canceling them."

"Why?" she demanded fiercely.

"Because it's going to be awkward." I didn't know how many times I had to tell her. "I made a move on my friend."

"And?" she annoyingly argued. "You should keep the date."

"Activity," I argued.

"Whatever. It's a date and before you shut me up, go on this date and have fun. Get out of your feelings."

I knew I wasn't so I listened to her babble.

"And when you're finished sucking---" I cut her off instantly. I didn't want to picture that in my head.

"Charley, it's not going to go that way."

"I was going to say...sucking on a lollipop. You know the

blow drops," she insinuated sarcastically.

"Really, Charley?"

Her infectious laughter filled the line. "Okay...okay." I could picture her rolling her eyes and cussing me out. "You should invite him to hang with us next weekend for my mama's fifty-six birthday party." Charlotte lived in Charlotte, North Carolina. Hence, the city.

"I'm not bringing Malcolm anywhere near y'all again. Y'all don't know how to act." We talked a few more minutes before the conversation veered to safer topics.

Malcolm would be here any minute now. He texted me that he was on his way thirty minutes ago. Despite trying all week, I couldn't find an adequate excuse to cancel on him. Every time I thought it was good, my inner voice chastised me. So I sucked it up. I anxiously pulled on strands of my hair while waiting for him to arrive.

The sudden sound of the doorbell ringing caused me to react. My insides danced with a nervousness I never had previously. I spun around, slipped on the long, yellow wool coat, and snatched my purse off the counter.

Opening the door, the rich scent of leather and vanilla mix drifted full-blown up my nose. I swallowed a lump in my throat. Malcolm's appearance was clean. He wore a yellow bomber jacket and paired it with dark jeans and brown boots. His hair was in a neat man bun at the nape of his neck.

His smile reached both corners of his lips. "Great minds think alike." He winked playfully.

My pupils journeyed down the length of his lean body and then back up to his thick eyebrows and peach fuzz.

"Ready?"

"Yeah," I pulled the door behind me after locking it with my forefinger and thumb.

"How's your week been?" he inquired subtly.

It felt like someone stuffed my mouth with cotton balls

since I couldn't formulate words. Side-eyeing Malcolm baffled me. I didn't know if he was being cordial or sarcastic because the Malcolm I knew addressed the situation and not let it slide which bothered me. If I had to be honest about the situation, my kisses were the bomb.

The thick soles of my boots clacked against the pavement as I answered, "Busy."

He held the passenger door, and I slid across his leather seats.

Walking around to his cobalt Maxima, I admired his figure. He carried himself with class. Today was going to be hard for us. It was almost like pretending to be someone else to enjoy the Saturday festivities.

He pushed to start the vehicle and hit his playlist, 'Friends.'

Arriving at the community's fall jubilee, we walked to the gate entrance. The older gentleman with graying hair and a face full of moles stamped the back of our hands as we entered.

"You're going to have people thinking we dressed alike on purpose," I joked, breaking the silence.

Malcolm didn't comment but gave me a lazy smile. Twisting my head toward the left, the Ferris Wheel caught my attention. I felt giddy on the inside as a little child would, jumping up and down. I clapped my hands eagerly and faced Malcolm. Squeezing my eyes briefly, I asked, "Where do you want to go first?" The volume of my voice elevated to a squeal. I expected him to agree with my decision.

"It doesn't matter."

"Well, since you said it like that, let's ride the Ferris Wheel." Malcolm was afraid of heights. I grabbed his hand and ushered him to the ride. He shook his head the entire time.

"Don't be a punk, Mal."

His head tilted at an arch. His dark gaze penetrated mine for the longest that a chill shot through my body.

"After this, we're going to wait until it gets dark to do the corn maze." He knew I was afraid of the dark.

"Unless I'm riding your back, you can forget it." I folded my arms over my breast as we stood in line at the Ferris Wheel.

"If I ride this thing, then we do the spooky corn maze," he reiterated.

Squinting my eyes and pursing my lips, I suggested, "If I get to jump on your back half way."

That pulled a smile from those gorgeous lips. "That's a bet."

"Let's shake on it," I teased, sticking my hand out.

He shook it as it was our turn to step up the stairs and onto the Ferris Wheel.

As soon as Malcolm sat on the ride, he quickly buckled himself, and I giggled. "You couldn't wait, huh?"

"Have you seen these things malfunction before?"

"Don't say that, Mal. We're stuck on this for now." I stuck my tongue out. His gaze landed on it. Reeling my tongue in, I glanced at the loving young couple waiting to catch the next seat. I did that to take my mind off how Malcolm looked at me. I was so confused right now. Did he feel something for me or not? I buckled my seatbelt as well. The ride attendant rechecked the seatbelts and pulled down the bar to secure us safely. He walked to the booth and pushed the button for the Ferris Wheel to move upward.

Malcolm grunted, gripping the bar forcefully.

I couldn't help but laugh again.

"Laugh now, but you're going to be crying later."

The corner of my mouth twisted, but my mind jumped in the gutter. Did he mean something else? Kicking my legs as the Ferris Wheel started moving, Malcolm moved closer to me as he wrapped an arm around my shoulders. I didn't want to open my mouth and make it even more awkward between us, so I let it be.

Enjoying the scenery of the evening as the ride went around three times before coming to a stop.

EIGHT

AUTUMN FUN

Malcolm

The night was young as friends enjoyed each others' company. The Ferris Wheel was a jump start to a fun evening as we climbed out of the ride. Aurora must have been feeling better as she grabbed my hand to lead me to the antique car show. We stopped in front of a '68 red Pontiac Firebird. It was decked out in the latest fashion with an updated GPS and sound system. The next stop was a classic '74 Oldsmobile Toronado with its original leather seats, original transmission, padded-vinyl roof, and steering wheel. The only upgrade it had was the radio system. We continued the surveillance of classic automobiles. Aurora oohed and awed at them.

"I'm getting hungry," she whined shortly.

I should have known she would say it. Shaking my head, we headed toward the BBQ food truck. We both ordered a pulled pork BBQ sandwich, a bag of funyuns, and a sweet tea.

Throwing away the empty containers, we strolled toward

the arts and crafts vendors. The evening sun started disappearing, and the night began to cool.

"We can't stay out here too long. It's getting cold," Aurora complained, grasping the collar of her coat with her hands as she shivered.

"It's not that cold yet."

"You're a man. You don't get cold like us."

"Start taking your vitamin B12s, Ds, and iron pills," I suggested as we headed forward. I caught her tongue sticking out. Sometimes, she was so childish which I preferred. "Come on, you know where we need to go next." I grabbed her arm and pulled her toward the corn maze before she had a chance to run away.

"We don't have to do this tonight."

"Ohh, yes, we do." The childish rumble spilling from my throat made Aurora stare at me, and it caused me to lose my balance, trekking across the grass.

"That's what you get," she teased, pointing down to the ground.

As she laughed at my expense, I grabbed her and started tickling her.

Her laughter was music to my ears. "Stop Mal... stop!" she yelled, trying to catch her breath. "Stop before you make me pee on myself in front of these people," she begged, laughing hysterically.

I released her, tilting my head to the side.

She shoved me in the chest. "That wasn't funny," she laughed herself.

"Bet." I nodded. "But you know what will be funny?" I asked wickedly, showcasing an enormous grin.

"What?"

"You running through the field."

"Ha ha, no it won't because I'll be on your back."

We bickered back and forth playfully as we stood behind a

group of people digging inside a wide bucket. Showing the dirty blonde attendant the orange band wrapped around our wrist, she offered us to take a flashlight or stated that the moon could lead us.

"Uh, uh, I'm grabbing a flashlight," Aurora said, passing me one. I slipped my wrist through the hoop on the small flashlight while Aurora held hers. We entered the corn maze and were graced with various Halloween decorations. We came across stacks of pumpkins throughout the maze, some decorated like Freddy Krueger, Chucky, Jason, goblins, and the nun's face hanging from a pole, among others. The decorations were spooky but also impressive.

As we walked deeper into the maze, we spotted a faux but comical cemetery. The graves were marked, 'Santa, the Easter Bunny, Relationships, real food, and the head of Jaws carved out of a giant white pumpkin. It was unique to see. Aurora took pictures every chance she got.

Coming to a dead end, we turned around and headed in another direction. The maze seemed to be getting more and more complex as we walked deeper into it. There was even a plastic tent sitting in the middle of the maze. We continued to walk, passing clowns, scarecrows, and the lady in the box from the movie, "Thirteen Ghosts."

My feet started to backpedal, but Aurora caught my wrist.

"I know you're not scared." The corner of her mouth curved wickedly.

"I'm not," I answered. "Don't want to get snatched up."

Not taking a chance, Aurora and I gave each other 'the look' and hurried to the other side of the tent. It was spooky enough with the moon out and these little flashlights not providing much comfort in the dark. Almost to the end of the course, I abruptly stopped.

Aurora bumped into me. "What's wrong, Mal?" she asked inquisitively, brows arched.

"I thought I saw something move over there." I pointed to the right.

Aurora wrapped her hands around my wrist, squeezing tight causing pain to shoot up my arm. "What did you see?" Her voice was shaky, peeking over her shoulder.

I had her where I wanted her before turning around and breathing onto her neck, "Your shadow!"

Aurora jerked back and hit me on the same arm. "You play too much. Let's go before I fight you out here."

Chuckling, I said, "Rory, you know you won't win, so let's go."

Having now completed the maze, I can say it was quite an experience. The maze spanned six acres.

"You made me walk the entire maze and I didn't ride on your back," she fussed, placing a hand on top of my shoulder. "Wait, I got something in my boot."

"You can ride it now," I expressed. When she didn't move, I glanced back at a flushed face. Scolding myself at the words I spoke made it awkward. I dipped so she could climb on my back. Carrying Aurora with ease, I made my way toward the car as we noticed other people leaving. Placing her on her feet, I pinched her cheek. "See...tonight was fun."

"Yeah, it was." She stood to the side as I held the door open. "I'm glad we came out and enjoyed each other's company as friends."

Closing the door, I strolled around the Maxima and slid behind the wheel. Before I made it to her place, Aurora was sound asleep. Pulling up to her place, I tapped her on the knee and she rolled over toward the window.

"Wake up, sleepy head. We're back at your place."

Aurora stretched her hands above her head. "Already, but I'm tired." She yawned, placing a hand over her mouth.

"That's why you're home."

"Yeah...yeah," she mocked.

"Don't forget the annual breast cancer function in two weeks."

"What time will it be? I may be late."

"Six. Do you want me to pick you up?" I asked, hoping she'd say yes. If she didn't want me to pick her up, then at least come to the function. I wanted my friend back.

"No, I'll make it. I know it's for your job."

"Okay, I'll see you then. Take care, Rory."

"You too, Mal."

Aurora opened the car door, and so did I. The routine was to escort her to her doorstep and wait for her to enter. She said goodbye with her lips, but her eyes expressed something else. Smiling, I nodded and pivoted back to my car. The vocal cords belonging to Ashanti had my mind spinning.

Tired wasn't the word I would use, more like exhaustion, but I spent it with my friend. A much-needed activity. She'd been avoiding me all week. I wouldn't put it past her to back out of the upcoming function in two weeks. I didn't know how she felt, but I had mixed feelings. Stepping inside my house, I kicked off my shoes and locked the door, putting on the alarm. The shower was calling my name. I stripped down and entered the warmth of the water. Minutes later, I lay under the covers. Tomorrow was a new day for worries.

NINE
YOU'RE MINE

Two Weeks Later

Every year, I conducted a charity ball for breast cancer awareness. It was to honor those who fought and were fighting the disease. As I handed over my keys to the valet, I glanced at the lavish pink carpet adorning the ground. My shoulders squared as I poked out my chest in gratitude. With a smooth stride, I admired the oversized balloon archway. To the left side of the hallway was a breast cancer table with more balloons and a bowl saying, 'grab one to get pinned'. I reached down, and one of the survivors pinned the symbol on the upper right side of the collar. I stepped into the ballroom immediately spotting my parents sitting at our assigned table. Nodding my head and putting up a finger, I strolled toward my employees and greeted them with their wives and significant others.

I checked my phone to see if Aurora texted, but she hadn't, so I made my way to my parents. My brother LaKeith couldn't make it due to a mandatory out of town meeting with the company. Leaning over, I kissed my mother on the cheek. "You look good, Ma."

"Thank you, son." Her smile reached both corners of her mouth, standing and twirling to give me a peek at what gripped her curvy body. The dress was a shiny black with a pink bowknot fashioned at the neckline.

Releasing her, I dapped my father's hand as he pulled me down for a manly hug. "You take after me." He winked, eyeing my attire.

"Thanks Pops." I pulled out the chair. "I see Mom had a helping hand in your outfit," I teased, skimming over his two-piece black suit and a floral pattern dress shirt.

"I dressed myself son." He chuckled, kissing my mother on the cheek.

Bobbing my head to his comic nature, I picked up the tall, plastic cup of ice water. Taking a sip and smacking my teeth, I grunted, "I need something stronger than this," pushing back from the table and asking my parents if they wanted something to drink.

Mom turned me down, but Pops commented, "Grab me a Long Island."

I walked toward the open bar and requested our drinks. Passing Pops his, I placed the plastic cup up to my lips and sipped on the crown and coke.

"So, is Rory coming tonight?" Mother asked me, fluttering her lids.

"Yes."

As they conversed, I sat pondering the objective for the night. Did I want to explore this thing we've been avoiding? My gut said yes, but her feelings came before mine. I looked down and realized the cup was empty. Strolling across the floor back to the bar and bobbing my head to the music, I requested a Whiskey Sour, thinking about the trip.

"Nice setup, Malcolm," a fellow employee said.

I nodded, lifting my drink and walking to the table. The decor of the Eiffel Tower centerpiece caught my eye with its ostrich feathers and pearls, illuminated by lights inside the tall vase. While in deep thoughts, my phone beeped. It was Aurora.

Aurora: Be there shortly.

Me: Take your time.

I wanted to type '*hurry up...can't wait to see you,*' but my thumb froze over the *h*. It was crazy to me that I wanted Aurora to know my feelings were more than just friendship.

Just last week, the absence of her came on strong. Thoughts of her voice echoing inside my house spooked me. The temperature in the house suddenly cooled. I paused and surveyed the living room, standing in the kitchen. Shaking my head, it was all mental. The realization was missing my friend. Closing the refrigerator, I had the urge to call her. My cell was lying on the coffee table when I seized it. Swiping up with my thumb, I scrolled to the favorites and paused, checking the date. It dawned on me she was with Charlotte for the weekend. A crooked grin etched the sides of my mouth, knowing I probably was the topic of her and Charlotte's conversation a time or two.

Ever since the festival, Aurora and I talked and texted less. I missed the friend in her. If I couldn't have Aurora as my woman, I was satisfied with the friend part, even if it hurt.

But what could it hurt if she knew? The thought of losing her made me frown. Maybe it was better if we kept things as they were and remained friends, I thought.

"You sure she's coming?" My father interrupted my private thoughts.

"She just texted."

Bouncing my head to "I Want You Around," I thought about my love life. There wasn't anyone in my life at the moment. I had dated a few women, but none of them were able to hold my attention for more than six months. The longest relationship lasted for two years. At that time, Aurora and I were both seeing someone.

Over the years, I one-sidedly compared them to Aurora. Whereas Aurora was thankful, the few I dated seldom showed gratitude for the things I did for them. Some women criticized simple places such as Olive Garden or visiting the zoo as a first date. Aurora would never.

When it was time to meet my parents after eight months of dating, I had a woman say *'that it was too soon'*. I side-eyed her and shook my head. Nope! If Aurora and I were out and I needed to drop by my parents, she was down.

The women were too money-oriented versus Aurora's sweet personality. She was entertaining and adventurous, and she encouraged me to do those things. She was classy with a little hood. She made my heart skip beats versus the women, causing sweat on the brows or curved lips when slick stuff came out of their mouths.

The few dates wanted me to plan everything from the flowers to picnics. On the flip side, Aurora showed her affection through subtle gestures, such as mentioning a restaurant to explore the food. She gifted me a yellow rose once, expressing it meant friendship. Those simple gestures meant a lot to me. It showed she cared about our friendship, even the flower. Over the years, having Aurora in my life, I tattooed her initials on the upper part of my thigh and below were words *'always my girl'*. Although she would never know unless we were intimate.

I picked up my cell and scrolled through Facebook. Something told me to look up and when I did, I noticed Aurora immediately. The hairs on the back of my neck ascended, and a warmness flowed through my chest. Her appearance blew me away, the way the V-neck midi magenta dress hugged her curves.

· · ·

"SHE'S HERE," I announced to my parents, but they were busy engaging in their own conversation. Involuntarily, my heart took off without me. I pushed back the chair and stood to my feet, tucking the chair under the table. I began the long mile walk to her when I noticed her glancing over her shoulder. My brows lifted in suspicion. Was she looking for me?

The closer I got, I stopped dead in my tracks recognizing her ex. Muscular frame, facial hair, four eyes, and a temple fade with bleached tips. He placed his large hands around her waist and jerked her closer, leaning down to kiss her neck. I made a beeline toward the bar and ordered the strongest drink. "Let me get a shot of Patron."

The bartender handed me the drink. Aurora, her date, and I made it to the table together. I could tell she was embarrassed.

"We made it." She blushed, her eyes surveying the table and smiling at my parents before locking eyes with me.

"It's so good to see you, Rory. I was wondering if you were going to keep Malcolm busy since LaKeith couldn't make it, but I see---" My mother left the conversation open.

Her eyes widened. "Where is LaKeith?" she asked my mother, but I answered roughly.

"Out of town." I smacked my teeth as I sipped on my Patron.

Aurora's eyes narrowed, then she twisted her head to the left. She patted her guest on the shoulder. "Everyone, this is Marshon. Malcolm." She gritted her teeth and lowered her lids.

I nodded and waved my hand. "Please have a seat." I started to pull out her chair, but Marshon stepped around and did. A plate of sliced chicken breast, mashed potatoes and gravy, and a side salad with a vinaigrette were placed in front of us.

Stepping back, I nodded and slid in beside her. I hated to admit it, but it made me angry. My jaw clenched, and a swish of heat emitted steam. The veins in my neck popped. I picked up the fork and played over the food, chewing a few bits of chicken. My chest puffed in and out angrily, scooping up the mashed potatoes and gravy. To help ease my emotions, I picked up my choice of liquor and placed it on my lips.

"Malcolm, why don't we go take a walk," I heard my father say. Replacing the drink on the table, I stood up and he clapped my back.

"You know I think it should be you on her arm tonight instead of him."

My head turned slightly to my father and he winked. "We've always known you had a crush on Rory. We thought the trip to Colorado pulled y'all closer. What happened?"

We ended outside the venue. "Nothing," I honestly answered.

"Well it should be you. I've never seen you shut down before since you're so outspoken. If being honest with yourself and Rory destroys the friendship, she isn't the one. But my heart is telling me that she is. She's fighting it. Don't allow your blessing to be blocked because you didn't speak on it." He patted my shoulders. "Now go get your woman." He started walking back inside the venue and I followed.

"I need a drink," I mumbled, pondering my father's viewpoint. At the bar, I requested two drinks and before I knew it, I handed the Amaretto Sour to Aurora.

Her brows furrowed, staring at the drink in front of her.

"Thank you, Malcolm," she called me by my first name, *strike one*. The Aurora I knew called my nickname anytime she could but not tonight.

Marshon grabbed the drink instead and slammed it against the table, drawing eyes to them. *Strike two!*

My gaze pierced him with disgust and he acknowledged with a scowl of his own.

"What are you drinking, Rory?" he asked.

I never took my sight away from him.

Aurora picked up the clear cup, placed it on her lips. "This is fine." She took a sip.

Marshon cut his eyes at me. "What are you drinking?"

"Amaretto Sour, her favorite drink that you should already know," I stressed, never taking my eyes off of him.

"I do," he snapped. *Strike three.*

Twisting my stance, I glanced at my father and he grabbed my mother's hand asking for a dance.

"I'm going to the bathroom." Aurora jumped up out of her seat and hurried off.

The second she stepped away, Marshon opened his mouth. "She's mine...for the night anyway," he professed sarcastically.

Still standing within earshot, I leaned forward and said calmly, "She may be yours for now...but she knows where her heart is." Smiling with my eyes, I sat down confidently in the chair.

Recognition dawned on his face. "See, I always knew you wanted her," he grunted. "Best friend, my ass."

My smirk grew wider.

"You're the reason we can't have a relationship."

I pointed my finger. "No, you're the reason why y'all can't have a relationship. You played with her heart instead of nurturing it. It's funny she has to come to me for simple things such as career decisions."

His jaws clenched.

Leaning forward with my elbows on the table, I highlighted, "When Aurora needed you, you gave her a lame excuse to stay at a dead-end job and continue to receive low pay. That job stressed her." I gritted my teeth. "She stayed until she couldn't take the verbal abuse anymore from her supervisors."

His lips parted, but I didn't give him time to reply as I raised a finger. Recalling a specific incident caused the heat from my neck to travel to my brain. "You also did not protect Rory's feelings when she cut off her father for coming at her sideways. You told her to suck it up and forget about him stealing money from her account. That's not the protection nor motivation she needs from her man." I used air quotes on the man part.

"But you do," he argued, his nostrils flared, and he squeezed his lips firmly.

"Actually, I do." I leaned back in the chair satisfied with my answer.

"Again, why would I do that when she had you in her corner like a love sick puppy?"

Sitting forward, I interlocked my fingers. "As her man, you should have stood your ground." I tossed back my drink, shooting darts at him.

Marshon's lips curved as he digested my words. With a sneer, he lifted the ice water and sipped. Facing me, he admitted, "You can't have Rory," he publicized before the sound of Aurora's heels graced us with her presence.

"There was a line." She looked between us. She must have felt the tension. "Shon, let's go dance." She placed her handbag on the table and grabbed his hand.

Marshon placed his hand in hers with a menacing smirk and walked away.

I clenched and unclenched my fist as my gaze followed them to the dance floor. Wasting no time, Marshon jerked her body to his and rested his hand on her butt.

Another reason why I disliked him was because he didn't respect boundaries. Finally pulling myself together, I found a partner to dance with. She was pretty with box braids and amber pupils, more on the golden side.

TEN

WE CROSSED THE LINE

Malcolm

There was a cheesecake with strawberry and blueberry compote at the table when I returned. Out of the corner of my eye, I felt Marshon's hateful glare. It amused me that he was jealous of our relationship. My parents finally made it back to the table to enjoy their dessert.

Their eyes locked with mine and I forced a daring smile. I stabbed the cheesecake a couple of times before marching to the bar requesting another drink. I was hitting all the hard liquor tonight.

A soft hand on the edge of my shoulder made me glance over my shoulder and stare into Aurora's highlighted eyebrows.

"What if I told you...you're too fine to be drinking yourself into a slumber?" Aurora asked the bartender for a bottle of water. She twisted the top and passed it to me.

Her concerns turned my frown into a smile. Staring into her eyes, I stated, "I didn't think you noticed with your ex on your arm twenty-four seven."

The corner of her mouth lifted. She pulled my hand, and we walked away from the bar. "I didn't have a choice. He came over and wouldn't leave."

My head snapped up. "Why didn't you call me, Rory?" Her name rolled off my tongue seductively and velvety.

Aurora's honey-brown eyes flickered with passion. Shaking her head, her voice softened. "I didn't want to mess up the evening with his foolishness."

"If he..." She placed a finger on my lips. "I know you, Mal." True, she did. She knew I would have raised hell over her. "We drove separately. He goes his way, and I go mine. He knows we're not getting back together. He just wanted to show you up."

I sighed, lowering my gaze on her lips. I parted my lips and licked her finger.

"Malcolm!" She jerked her finger away. I meant for it to be sexual. "See, it's time for you to put down the liquor." She flicked her wrist. "Go ahead and drink your water so we can get a dance in for the night."

I nodded, accepting her statement. I had to make a run to the bathroom. Returning to the ballroom, I noticed Marshon smothering Aurora's chair and whispering inside her ear.

"Ready to dance, Rory?" I extended my hand as two pairs of eyes raised towards me.

"She's with me." Marshon slimy hands wrapped tightly around her shoulders.

"And who's going to stop me." My tone was low enough for his ears as I rolled my eyes, daring him. Although I was chilled, it didn't mean that I couldn't lay hands.

Marshon clenched his fist, eyed me then my father, before removing his arm, and frowning.

Aurora extended long, silky legs, standing taller than her average height in black heels. Her manicured nails intertwined with mine and her eyes sparkled with mischief.

"I'm out." Marshon pushed back from the table and jumped to his feet.

I tucked Aurora's arm under mine without acknowledging his dismissal. Giving Aurora a spin on the dance floor, she raised her hands behind my neck and interlocked her fingers to "Make Love to Me". Listening to the lyrics by Luke James, I dropped my hands to her lower back and pressed her closer. We swayed to the rhythm of the beat. The tempo had me in a zone as the song was clear to me. I wanted more time with my best friend, forever, if I could have it. I was making a move whether it enhanced our friendship or not.

"I want to make sure you get home safely." Lowering my head, I kissed the top of her forehead.

Aurora's eyes darkened with a smile. Shaking her head, she grabbed my hand. We said our goodbyes to my parents, and I thanked everyone for coming out to support the foundation.

This was the moment, but why was I second-guessing myself? *Am I doing the right thing? Should we cross this line? There's no going back if I could pretend.* Not realizing I'd talked aloud for five minutes, I looked up into Aurora's flowing hair.

"Are you going to sit in your car or do you want coffee to sober up?"

I shut off the engine and jumped out, entering her place. Slipping out of my shoes, I set them by the door and sat on her sofa, picking up the remote.

"I'm going to go take off this dress. You're home...go make a cup. You know where everything is." Her voice lingered, and my lids lowered.

One minute, I was fixing coffee, and the next, I was in her bedroom. Our gaze locked.

Aurora gasped, placing her hand over her heart. "Malcolm--"

I moved quickly and covered my lips over hers. I half

expected her to shove me off, but her arms wrapped around my neck. With the speed of lightning, I quickly removed my hot pink blazer, unbuttoned my shirt, and discarded my pants.

As I unraveled the towel, my eyes were drawn to Aurora's shapely body, thick thighs and tight waist. Her breasts were full. A lazy smile fell as she scooted toward the headboard. She laid down, squirming and touching herself, beckoning to come with her index.

Witnessing Aurora being sexual towards me penetrated my heart with a demand to protect what was mine. Licking my lips, I climbed onto the bed, stopping at the apex of her center and working my way deep inside her heart.

The sounds of lovemaking went beyond the moon and the stars. Her vocals and my moans blended well into the wee hours of the night. Her light snores were music to my ears. I'd cherish them for years to come.

My breathing started slowing. *I've made love to my Rory,'* was the last thing I remembered. The morning after was awkward as I found myself alone in her bed, reaching out and feeling a space. I called for her, "Rory! Rory!" as I rubbed the sleep from my eyes. There was no response, so I flipped back the covers and rolled out of bed, pulling on my boxers and then pants. I felt uneasy as I swung open the bedroom door and searched for Aurora. My heart fell out of my chest and shattered into a million pieces.

She was nowhere in her house.

"Damn," I cursed, using other expletives and hitting my palm against the countertop. That's when I saw a note taped to the refrigerator.

Aurora: Gone to church. Didn't want to wake you. I'll text you later.

Running a hand down my face, I sat down on her bar stool and hung my head. We crossed a line we couldn't take back. I wondered if Aurora regretted her decision.

AURORA

AS MUCH AS I thought it would be strange to sleep with my best friend, I was pleasantly surprised. Lying next to him and hearing light snores produced a heartfelt smile. Tracing his lips with my finger, I leaned forward and placed my lips on his. He didn't wake but stirred a little. As I breathed in his musky cologne, I realized why I wasn't grossed out. I was in love with my bestie. My eyes ballooned out of my head. My heart hammered in my chest. *Wait, I have to get out of here.* Rolling away from him, I slid a leg out and then the other as I tiptoed in the bathroom to take care of my hygiene. Quietly twisting the knob to the bathroom door, I prayed Malcolm was still asleep. I pulled it open and thanked God he was.

Throwing on a pair of leggings and a sweatshirt, I left a handwritten note and attached it to the refrigerator with the turtle magnet he gave me when he visited Hilton Head, a few years back. That pulled another grin as I scrambled to grab my keys from the bowl in the middle of the island. The realization hit me again, and I felt so guilty. My stomach dropped, my cheeks glowed with heat, and my knees wobbled while I stuck my feet into a pair of shoes. Easing out the front door, I drove to Dunkin to grab a medium, hot Turtle latte to calm my nerves.

After the first couple of sips, my senses came back. *How could I sleep with my best friend? Why did I sleep with him? Was I that drunk to tell him no?* I hit my fist against the wheel, driving back to my place and noticing his car parked. Not facing the issues as I should have, I ran...well drove away.

Drove to a park and sat on the bench facing a brown and black mama duck and her babies waddling in the pond. *Babies? Did I want babies?* I knew from previous conversations

Malcolm wanted kids. But me...well...for the sake of last night, there was a strong possibility I could be someone's mama in the near future. And to top it off, I was ovulating. "Way to go, Rory," I grunted, rolling my eyes and sighing in frustration.

The morning air gave a slight chill as the trees rustled over my head. I shivered, placing one hand between my thighs and the other holding my morning caffeine. As thoughts ran wild, I concluded that I couldn't fight these feelings.

"I'm in love with Malcolm," I hissed breathlessly. "With Mal. My best friend," I confessed, confirming it out loud. "Damn, I'm in love with Malcolm." I slapped a hand over my forehead and sighed.

There was no point in arguing why he was the one for me as I counted on my fingers. We held mutual respect for one another's beliefs. I trusted him with my whole heart and then some. He wasn't selfish. He spent quality time with me. Malcolm always came to the needs of others despite being busy. Malcolm was an all-around guy, dependable and honest.

In the past, I subconsciously compared my exes to Malcolm. I assumed I failed in those relationships, but it wasn't me. It was the men. They weren't my best friend.

Like Marshon, he had the qualities of being a good man, but he wasn't supportive enough for my needs. He didn't speak life into me as Malcolm had. He was worried about Malcolm and not fulfilling his needs for me. Another example where I remembered comparing the likes of them. I recalled being sick over the weekend. And since I was the girlfriend, I called Marshon first because he was my man. Of course, he gave me some sorry excuse as to why he couldn't come that Saturday. He was on his way out of town with his best friend Demontrey.

The thing was, he hadn't left his house. He could have stopped by on his way out, but he flat-out told me no. So I called my bestie. Malcolm nursed me back to health with chicken noodle soup and ginger ale. Another occasion,

Malcolm brought me ice cream when I was cramping and didn't feel like getting out of bed. Not only the minor things, but he advised me to leave my dead-end job at the hospital to pursue a better position and better pay. Malcolm has contributed to my needs unselfishly.

My eyes widened, and I realized the person I was looking for was right in front of me all along.

But you can't have him. I know I can't have him. Yes, I was talking to myself. I needed advice. Thinking of what we did messed with my head, causing an ache in the frontal lobe. We've crossed the line of no return. Standing to my feet, I sat behind the wheel and turned on the heat to the lowest setting.

Needing to hear sound advice and steer me away from my guilty conscience, I dialed Charlotte's number from the Bluetooth on the dashboard.

"Morning, Rory!" Charlotte's voice sounded rushed like she was doing her morning walk.

"Are you walking?"

"Yeah, I'm on my fourth lap around the block."

"I...I can call you back," I stuttered anxiously.

"Nope you called so it must be important."

"Charley, I call you in the mornings."

"Yeah, but it sounds urgent. What's up." The sound of the wind wooshing and cars beeping could be heard on her end.

I blurted out, "Talk some sense into me."

"About getting it on with Malcolm?"

"Charley, I didn't call you for that! I need serious help." Mumbling under my breath, I guiltily stated, "I've already slept with him."

Charley screamed in my ear. "When? When did it happen?"

"Last night."

"Well, I'll be damned. You done slept with the bestie." Her laughter was filled with sarcasm.

"And it was wrong," I berated, looking straight ahead.

"No, it wasn't. I told you y'all were a couple at the reception. I knew it," she cheered on, advising me that it was okay to be with the love of my life.

"I'm embarrassed," I stressed. "We crossed the friendship line. I don't know how I can stand to look at him like a friend. I don't know if we're still friends."

"Why would you want to be friends with Malcolm?"

Her question offended me. "What do you mean?"

"The friendship is over between y'all. You need to snatch up your man, Rory," she rambled. "I can't believe you called me for advice not to hook up with Mal. Remember I told you guys that y'all were more than friends."

"So I'm not crazy for sleeping with him?"

"No, Rory. I've seen you in relationships. None of those men compared to what you and Malcolm have. I met him once at the reception and could tell there was more to it than meets the eye. I swear to God, I saw it in his." Her voice was animated, witty, and vibrant. "Yours was wishy-washy, but after that dance, your body language expressed what your mouth couldn't. And you can't blame it on the a...a...alco...hol," she sang, reiterating many times before I could reply.

"Char---"

She cut me off. "I know I may be overstepping my boundaries, but when's the official date? Are you going to let him plan the evening? Wait, I bet he already knows your likes and dislikes."

Sighing, I admitted what she already knew.

"Hold on Rory, let me get on this sidewalk. There's a car behind me," she informed me. "Okay, I'm back."

"We're supposed to meet up later this week for game night at one of his home boys' house. But I'm not going to make it."

"Why not?" she challenged.

I bit my bottom lip. "Um, have you not heard anything I've been saying."

She corrected me. "Rory, you are a thirty-three-year-old, single woman who happened to have sex with her best friend and it probably was the best." Her uncontrollable laughter struck a nerve because it was. "Spare me the details. Like I was saying, you shouldn't allow sex to break up y'all outing. You act like you don't know how to play the funk in front of friends because you sure do in front of family," she scolded motherly.

Maybe I called the wrong person to talk sense into me. I hissed and rolled my eyes. "You don't understand, Charley."

"I do, but do you boo." She paused thoughtfully," "Oh, my plans have changed. I'm coming down for Thanksgiving. I've convinced Mama to come with me."

In mild shock, I asked, "What about your sisters?"

"RiRi is going with her boyfriend's family to Raleigh. Alexandria and the kids are staying here with her husband. So, me and Mama coming. And you better make your sweet potato pie."

I giggled, shaking my head. "I got you girl. I guess I'll see you in three weeks."

Ending the call, I didn't return home. Instead, I went to Walmart to buy time, hoping he left when I returned home. Two hours later, Malcolm's car was gone. My heart sank, but I lifted my head and carried three bags of miscellaneous items inside.

ELEVEN
GIVING THANKS

Three Weeks Later

After three weeks of missing my friend, my only friend, the bestie, I've been miserable. I caused it myself by not fixing the problem, but by hiding from it. Moping around the house and refusing to leave the bed unless it was work time was the norm.

As I recalled the situation, all I could think about was that we ruined our friendship. What true friends experience mind-blowing, amazing sex with one another? None that I knew of. And that guilt alone weighed heavily, but I also missed him.

Like a friend worried about the other, Malcolm did reach out. I, on the other hand, declined his calls and texts. He had a key to my house, but he wasn't the type to drop by unless I gave him the okay.

I pulled in front of my childhood home and entered the one-story ranch-style house. At the door, I heard soft R&B music and knew it was playing from the kitchen. As I entered the house, a strong fragrance greeted my senses. It smelled sweet but manly. Something like vanilla, cashmere, and woodsy. Mama lit a Thanksgiving candle every year. Strolling toward the candle, I read, 'Warm and Welcome.'

"Hey, Mama, I can smell the greens over this candle." I leaned forward and kissed her on the cheek.

"You know this is how I get down in my kitchen." Her smile was as big as the Autumn sun. "I have the water on for your sweet potatoes."

Pulling back from her hug, I skimmed Mama's outfit. A pair of pants and a regular shirt. Pre-Thanksgiving dinner, she wore raggedy clothes before looking presentable.

Angling my head, I caught wind of words written on her apron. There was a drawing of God's sun shining bright and the scripture from 1 Chronicles 16-34, 'Oh give thanks to the Lord, for he is good; for his steadfast love endures forever!' The corner of my lips curved. Mama always wore a spiritual or funny apron yearly.

Mama returned the gesture, noticing me reading her apron. "One year, I'm going to get you one." She winked, patting my arm.

"Thank you, Ma. Where's Poppa Terry?" I asked about my stepfather.

Mama nodded toward the backyard. "Outside frying the turkey."

"Okay, I'll go speak before I get started alongside you." I exited through the screen door. My stepfather, Terry, was of average height. He had a full, grey beard and no hair on top of his head. His skin was the color of smooth honey. "It smells good out here, Poppa Terry."

"Hey, baby girl." He closed the lid to the turkey and pivoted, stretching his muscular arms wide. "It's good to see you." His eyes sparkled.

"Good to be home for the holiday." We chatted awhile before I stepped back inside to help Mama.

Mama and Terry changed into their Thanksgiving outfits to sit in the living room talking with friends and family while I slid the last sweet potato pie out of the oven.

"Hey, cousin!" Charlotte's voice echoed over the music.

Setting the hot pie on the table, I removed my hand from the mitten. Spinning around, I hugged her. "I see y'all made it."

She side-eyed me and pulled back. "You know I wouldn't miss the gathering." Her grin stretched so far that I saw all thirty-two teeth. "It sure smells good in here."

"Right, Mama and Poppa Terry did that."

Family and friends entered the house as Poppa Terry finished saying grace. Charlotte stood behind me fixing her plate and leaned in, "So, am I going to see Mr. Malcolm tonight?"

"I don't know. I haven't seen or talked to him since then."

"Rory, you haven't talked to Malcolm!"

I pivoted and placed a finger on my lips. "Shh!"

She shrugged, nodding.

"We'll talk about that later."

The doorbell rang...

"Hey, how's it going?" The voice belonging to a certain someone paused me in motion as my eyes followed the voice standing inside the living room. Our gazes locked instantly. I swallowed a lustful, nervous gasp. Malcolm looked good. The dark wash jeans and tan turtleneck had me drooling. He paired it with the brown boots along with a black trench coat. He knew trench coats on a man did something to me. I couldn't take my eyes off him as he talked with a cousin of mine. After he greeted everyone in the living and family room, Poppa Terry told him to fix a plate.

"Charlotte, come here," I whispered, placing my plate on the end of the counter and pulling her away from the macaroni.

"Rory!" she fussed.

"He's here."

Her head lifted with a gleam in her eye. "Malcolm?"

"Yes, and he's coming in here."

She gave me a push in his direction. "Go talk with your man."

"Char---"

"Good evening ladies." Malcolm's tone was profound as his gaze lingered on me in the corner.

Charlotte with her fast tail, spun around, smiling from ear to ear, placing her oversized plate on the table and rushed toward him.

"It's good to see you again." She reached in for a hug, and he reciprocated, not taking his eyes off me. "I know today will be even better since you're here. Make sure you make my girl scream your name later." She winked, and I gasped dramatically, causing others to look.

Charlotte turned around and grabbed her plate. "I'll catch up with you later, Rory." She returned to the macaroni and placed a hefty amount onto the heavy plate.

No one was standing in the kitchen except for me and Malcolm.

My voice quivered. "Do you want me to fix your plate?" My head hung low. As friends, we never fixed one another plate, so I didn't understand why I asked that question.

Malcolm didn't comment but moved closer to me. I inhaled deeply as his eyes lowered to my lips. His right hand lifted and fingered my cheek. The hunger started in my mind and sent a signal to every lady part of my body. "Can we go somewhere to talk in private?"

Nodding, I grabbed his hand and rushed down the hall into my old bedroom.

"I know what we did felt wrong, but it wasn't. It was right on so many levels."

"Malcolm---" I started to say, but he put his hand under my chin and tightened his lips.

I closed my mouth with a daring smile. That was his serious look.

"We've avoided this conversation too long. You know by now this situation would have been dealt with, but I took your feelings into consideration. To allow you to reflect and come to a conclusion about us. And yes, there's an us." His obsidian orbs radiated, penetrating deep within mine. "We've crossed the lines of friendship and entered into a soul-tie connection." He moved even closer, chest to face. "I've loved you my whole life, hiding my feelings just for you. This awkwardness we've been giving for the last month was what I wanted to avoid. Now, I'm putting my feelings first as well. I want you. I want to put my love inside of you. I want to hear your sweet cries through the night, in the mornings, and in the daytime." He licked his lips, and I gasped, breast rising and falling at the sound of every word he professed. "I want us to explore this loveship." His gaze deepened in passion.

Lifting my head, I spoke softly and stepped back to breathe. "I'm scared."

"I understand."

I put my hand on his chest. The rhythm pulsed in sync with mine. "I've known for a while too, but I didn't want it to be like it is now. After we slept together, it brought so many emotions in me that I had to spend that time alone to collect my true feelings." My eyes misted. "There's only been you in front of me all this time. I'm willing to try this loveship," I teased, pursing my lips. "But if this doesn't work out, our friendship will be over."

"Rory, I already know you. And some things I don't like that get on my nerves, but I'm yours."

I countered quickly. "And that's mutual. Because I hate the way you smack, sucking on ribs as you lick your fingers."

Malcolm's pupils danced playfully before they burned with passion, grabbing both sides of my face and lowering his lips onto mine. The kiss started off innocent but transformed into hunger, arms wrapped around heads and back and breathing uncontrollable. The demanding moans coming from our mouths ended up as we collapsed across the bed until the banging on the door jerked us apart.

"Y'all coming out to eat, or is Malcolm eating in there?" Charlotte's laughter was high-powered and rowdy. She lightly tapped the door before stepping away.

Malcolm glanced at me. "Ready to eat?"

Biting my bottom lip, I nodded and pecked his lips before moving toward the door. I twisted the doorknob and smoothed the wrinkles in my dress before heading to the kitchen to reheat my plate.

MALCOLM

I ALLOWED Aurora to leave the room before making my presence known. As I rounded the corner, several pairs of eyes met mine.

"You good, Malcolm," her cousin Bobby asked, the corner of his lip curved.

"Yeah, I'm good. The food is this way right." I pointed toward the kitchen, and he shook his head smiling.

Throughout dinner, Aurora and I kept an intense eye connection sitting across the table from one another.

Aurora's mother announced that we'll be participating in a Thanksgiving game shortly. Charlotte thought it best if Aurora and I sat next to each other as she offered up her seat.

"Hey...hey, put the TV on mute fellas, and participate," Aurora's mother said, standing in the center of the family room, holding a sheet of paper. Some stood to their feet, others twisted in their seats, and a few joined the dining table. "It's called 'Table Talk'. We're going to go around the room and say why we're thankful and answer some other questions. I'll start with 'Use a word to describe this family'."

"Loving. Understanding. Loud. Crazy. Funny. Accommodating. Countretto," went around the room.

"What's Coun...tretto?" Aurora's mother asked in confusion, her eyebrows lifted and head twisted at an angle.

"It's country and ghetto," one of the kids hollered and everybody fell in laughter afterwards.

"I see we're never too old to learn. Now---" Her eyes scanned the room and landed on no one in particular. "---What is something you're grateful for?"

"Thankful for family, good food, these drinks Rory created for us," her cousin, Eddie, announced, raising a plastic cup filled with a light orange color.

Everyone roared in a hearty chuckle.

"I'm thankful I'll be retiring in less than a year...thankful for my beautiful wife of sixteen years, a beautiful daughter, and hopefully grandchildren in the near future." Poppa Terry winked at us, kissing his wife on the cheek.

Aurora and I found ourselves at the center of attention as the room erupted into a frenzy, with fingers being pointed in our direction.

"Wait a minute, now," she started to say, but Charlotte cut her off.

"Girl, we know what's up." She faced me and a wicked grin slipped across her face. "Malcolm, are you thankful for anything?"

She put me on blast. Rubbing a hand down my face as I sat beside my best friend, I turned to face her. "Well, I know everyone knows or will know but Aurora and I---"

"Are you pregnant?" Her mother shouted excitedly.

Aurora jumped to her feet. "Mama...what! No....no!"

That pulled a deep rumble from the back of my throat. I knew it would happen eventually. Yes, I wanted kids with my best friend. Standing to my feet since her family made it obvious, I took Aurora's left hand and rubbed my thumb across her smooth knuckles. "Rory," I started as she slowly slid into the chair. "Rory, I've told you already, but we're moving out of the friend zone and beginning a relationship. These past weeks have been miserable without you. Your absence consumed my thoughts. Couldn't sleep, tossing and turning during the night. I even daydreamed about hearing your voice in my head."

"Aww," someone said.

"I'm thankful to God that he placed you in my life a long time ago. A time when we needed each other but didn't know we needed one another. The lost, skinny woman looking for her class. When I saw you, I knew we'd click. We've been together since then as besties." I imitated her signature sign with my two fingers.

Someone chuckled.

Never taking my eyes off Aurora, I reached behind my back and inside my back pocket, fidgeting for the ring I'd held onto for a while. "Rory, I need you as my plus one forever and ever. Will you marry me?"

Gasps and praises went around the room as tears pricked the corner of Aurora's honey-brown eyes. Both of her hands trembled, the other going over her mouth. Pushing back the chair, I kneeled and pulled out a diamond-cut engagement ring. I slipped it on her hand, piercing her with a questionable brow. She nodded her head, tears streaming down her face. Lifting to my feet, I kissed her with a need.

"That's how you end Thanksgiving...with a bang! Congratulations, Rory and Malcolm!" Charlotte screamed at the top of her lungs.

Congratulations went around the room again. For the rest of the evening, my best friend...my woman sat alongside me as we watched a football game on the big screen as a family while her mother started slicing the sweet potato pie and cutting red velvet cake for dessert.

My dessert was Aurora as she lay nude underneath me. Loving Aurora was a precious gift from God indeed. We experienced galaxies behind the naked eye while exploring each others' bodies as one. There was no other woman but Aurora for me. My Thanksgiving ended well...so well that...

EPILOGUE

A year later

Aurora wore my last name, Brown, for the past year as a happily married wife and mother to our one-year-old daughter, Ariyn. We were still in love as friends first and then as parents. Our one-year-old daughter, Ariyn, was a bubbly little girl. Her personality came from Aurora, but she looked like the girl version of me. Currently, her hair was in two pigtails. She finally learned to sit still while watching her mother getting ready at the last minute. We were on our way to my parents since we spent last year with hers.

"I got the diaper bag." I stood up, picked up the scattered hair bows, and placed them into its container. Peeking over my shoulder, I asked, "Do you need me to get anything else, Rory?"

She snatched her shoulder bag from the side chair. "Nope, I think I got everything."

Scanning my wife's figure, I adored every curve and stretch mark she gained after having Ariyn. Aurora gave me half of her. Our gaze connected and with hunger, I bit my bottom lip. Smiling, she shook her head.

I was head over heels for her and didn't dare ask her to return to her pre-baby weight. Nor did I want her to. When I said, I do. I meant forever and ever.

Ariyn handed for Aurora, but I snatched her up as we loaded into Aurora's brand new SUV, a Kia Selto, which I'd bought for her recently.

The ride to my parents wasn't far, thirty minutes tops. Listening to an R&B station, I glimpsed out the side of my vision. Aurora leaned against the window. She was probably on her way to sleep. A smirk slipped from my face as I thought how blessed I was as a man. I had the love of my life, a child, a family who loved us and who was willing to help every step of the way. This Thanksgiving, I was getting a double portion of my blessings.

Hearing light snores caused my heart to swell with love, side-eyeing my wife. I placed my hand over hers as we cruised along the street. Pulling into my childhood home, I noticed my brother beat me there. Opening the car door and reaching into the back seat, I pulled Ariyn from her car seat and grabbed the diaper bag. Before I knocked, my mother answered the door with a smile on her round face, stretching her arms wide.

"Hey, my babies," she said.

I passed her Ariyn as I kissed her on the cheek, handing over the bag.

Mother glanced over my shoulder. "Y'all ain't get no rest last night?" she implied, raising her brows and shaking her head in humor.

I didn't respond as I spun around to grab my sleeping wife from the car. Tapping on the glass, Aurora's eyes widened sleepily. She rubbed her eyes and grunted, "I'm sleepy, Mal. Can't I go back home and sleep?"

Holding the door open, I slid my hand around her waist and unbuckled her seat belt. Carefully grabbing her and leading her out of the car, I placed a kiss on her lips. "Later you can sleep all you want," I promised her with a wink.

Aurora grabbed her purse and gripped my hand as we stepped inside the one-brick-story home.

"Hello everyone," Aurora spoke to my parents, greeting them with a kiss on the cheek and a hug.

"Damn, y'all trying to be like Russel and Ciara," LaKeith joked, wrapping his arms around Aurora into a hug, rubbing her round belly. He released her and grinned at me. "I see you ain't wasting no time."

We dapped and hugged, teasing each other as we waited for Mama to finish preparing the side dishes as my father carved the fried turkey. While waiting, I asked Aurora if she could make her signature beverage. Her drink was a hit last fall, and it was good. My father kept a bevy of liquor around the house, so she agreed.

Aurora was quick with the concoction since she complained of being tired. My brother and I drank the hot apple cider mixed with Jack Daniel's fire whiskey concoction while she nursed the mocktail version. Time seemed to fly as we watched the Falcons lose by ten points.

After dinner, Mama served a brown sugar caramel pound cake and placed it in the middle of the table.

Aurora suddenly got up and entered the kitchen, coming back with a chocolate-covered dome set on a plate. On the bottom was scribbled, 'Happy Thanksgiving bestie, my plus one for life' as she set it down in front of me.

Aurora smiled before returning to the kitchen. This time she held a cup in her hand with some brown liquid.

"What's this?" I asked with confusion because I thought I was going to get a slice of the pound cake. Maybe the drizzle was for the cake, I presumed. The way Aurora's pupils dilated had me questioning her motives as she eased toward me. But if my baby wanted me to have this dessert, I'd eat it for her. She handed me the cup of steaming liquid.

"Wait, let me get some pictures of the dome." She strolled to the living room and grabbed her phone, snapping away.

"You made this?"

"Yes, I've been trying to perfect my skill."

Facing her, my mind began to turn. "How did you get it over here? Or did you make it in the kitchen?"

She slapped my shoulder. "No, Mal. I didn't just make it. I made it yesterday and brought it over here since I knew we were coming for dinner."

I nodded.

"Okay, all you have to do is pour the hot caramel over the dome."

"Is something inside of it?"

"Pour the caramel, man," LaKeith anxiously hollered.

Shaking my head, I began to pour the liquid. The dome started to melt instantly, creating a crater at the top and falling inward like an earthquake swallowing the earth's surface.

My eyes widened at the pink and blue foot. Angling my head, I stared into my wife's curved smile. "We're having twins?"

"Yes," she answered as praises erupted in the house, scaring Ariyn in the process. Jumping to my feet, I kissed my wife passionately on the lips.

"Hey...hey now...you're in my house," Mama said, crying tears of joy.

"We're having twins, Mal."

So when I said I was receiving two portions of a blessing, I didn't know it was this. But I was ready for the challenge. I had my plus one, and now I was blessed abundantly. From besties to my forever lady.

The End!

AFTERWORD

Whew!! I made it! I finished! Thank you, God! Thank you again, readers, for giving me a chance on this sweet romance. Truthfully, I wasn't able to write thanks to writer's block. I was inspired by a recent trip to the mountains, Colorado, and the wedding, but everything else is made up.

Was the ending expected? Did you enjoy this novella? If so, leave a message/comment/review/note on Amazon, Facebook, Instagram, or Goodreads. You can follow me on those platforms as well. Look for S. Cassadera.

ALSO BY S. CASSADERA

Christian Fiction

The Predatory Pastor

Wolves in Sheep's Clothing

The Fraudulent Psalmist

Trials & Tribulations

Enduring the Trials

Contemporary Romance

Falling For You

Love is Saying I'm Sorry

Love on a Bet

Smitten by a Cowboy

Her Life as She Knew It

Second Time Coming

Entanglement of Love Stories

Arranged by Fate

ABOUT THE AUTHOR

Fun fact about me

I'll write a book and think it's finished until these side characters start talking. For instance, I wrote 'Wolves in Sheep's Clothing' thinking it was done, and then a year later, another character had something to say. Now, 'The Fraudulent Psalmist' is out. Oh, by the way, y'all might want to check out my thought-provoking Christian Fiction collection. Yeah, not only do I write romance, but that genre, too. So, yeah, that's me. I flip-flop between these two genres. I'm trying to dive into thriller/suspense next. So look in the future for a book. Who knows, it may be two, depending on y'all's review and engagement.

Once again, thank you for taking this journey with Aurora and Malcolm. I hope their story caused your heart to flutter or think about gathering the family for the holidays. We are all we have left.

Last but not least: ways to support me!

1. Share my work
2. Tell someone about the book/word of mouth
3. Recommend my work
4. Buy the book
5. Tag me on social media
6. Recommend my books to your library

7. Engage with me in my reading group by joining: S. Cassadera's Reading Group @ https://www.facebook.com/groups/321975449941124/
8. Join my newsletter: https://mailchi.mp/34c9ee026d73/authorscnewsletter

Until next time, Happy Thanksgiving!

MAJOR KEY
PUBLISHING

Nov. 30th!

I CAN
make you
LOVE ME

NADIA NICOLE

amazon.com

Be sure to check out our other releases:
www.majorkeypublishing.com/novels

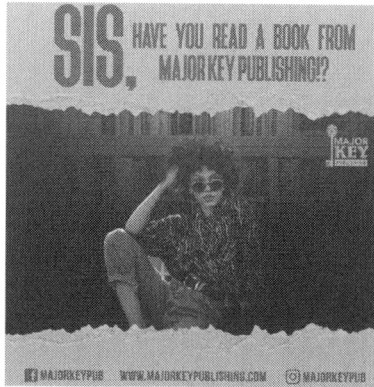

To submit a manuscript to be considered, email us at
submissions@majorkeypublishing.com

MAJOR KEY

Major Key Publishing is accepting submissions
from experienced & aspiring authors
in the areas of :
Contemporary Romance, Urban Fiction, Paranormal,
Mystery & Suspense, Christian Fiction & New Adult
Romance!

If interested in joining a successful, independent publishing
company, send the first 3-5 chapters of your completed
manuscript to submissions@majorkeypublishing.com
SERIOUS INQUIRIES ONLY!

WWW.MAJORKEYPUBLISHING.COM

Be sure to LIKE our Major Key Publishing page on Facebook!

Made in the USA
Las Vegas, NV
02 March 2025

18952231R00061